High Octane

USA Today Bestselling Author
Ashley Zakrzewski

Copyright © 2022 by Ashley Zakrzewski

All rights reserved.

No part of this book may be reproduced in any form or by any electronic or mechanical means, including information storage and retrieval systems, without written permission from the author, except for the use of brief quotations in a book review.

Contents

Chapter 1	1
Chapter 2	7
Chapter 3	13
Chapter 4	19
Chapter 5	25
Chapter 6	31
Chapter 7	37
Chapter 8	43
Chapter 9	49
Chapter 10	53
Chapter 11	57
Chapter 12	59
Chapter 13	63
Chapter 14	67
Chapter 15	71
Chapter 16	77
Chapter 17	81
Chapter 18	89
Chapter 19	95
Chapter 20	101
Chapter 21	107
Chapter 22	111
Chapter 23	117
Chapter 24	121
Chapter 25	127
Chapter 26	131
Chapter 27	137
Chapter 28	143
Chapter 29	147
About the Author	151

Chapter One

She's hated *this* man since the moment she laid eyes on him.

Callie admits this only to herself. During sessions of intense bikram, as they frown upon outward expressions of anger at the Asana Peace and Serenity yoga studio and the instructors believe in good vibes only.

I mean, you know, you could be *mindful* of your anger, but don't fucking overdo it or anything. God forbid.

The thing is, *this* dude has the outrageous ability to always take the last shot of barley grass at the Jamba Juice next door. It had become a *thing*. Like, in the last month, this happened at least five times. Maybe she should start going to sunrise hatha sessions. Early bird gets the barley grass?

He'll clunk around like some sort of fucking rhinoceros, his huge gym bag always knocking shit over. He wears obscene muscle tees to show off his enormous biceps, and those ridiculous jersey shorts year-round, even in the dead of winter when it was only forty degrees out.

And it was happening . . . fucking . . . *again*. This morning. She slept through her alarm, because Instagram models who wake up at 5:30am to do pilates down by the pier are kidding themselves.

"We're out of barley grass, ma'am," the flustered teenager behind the counter tells Callie. The teenager's eyes flick to the man standing over by the pickup station. "Another customer just ordered our last shot."

Callie follows the worker's gaze and narrows her eyes at the absolute leviathan standing by the counter. She swears under her breath.

"That's fine, it's not your fault," she reassures the worker, who gives her a grateful smile. "I'll have the whey shake instead, for now."

Callie has *had* it. She stomps over to the pickup counter and glares up at the bane of her existence.

She's seen this man many times before, but never up close, and only now notices how there's a mole there, to the left of his nose, and another one, above his right eyebrow. He's not conventionally attractive, by any means. His nose is large, angular. He's so . . . broad. Wait. Why does she care if he's attractive or not? She breathes through her nostrils. Focus. Come back to center.

He glances down at her, shifting his attention from the iPhone in his hand. The man was playing a game of Candy Crush.

"What?" he asks, offended by the strength of her gaze.

"Stop," she says through her teeth, "taking my *fucking* barley grass."

His stance shifts. He finds he's taken aback by this young woman, almost half a foot shorter than him, dressed in Lululemon with a pink yoga mat slung over her back, cursing at him about barley grass.

This was not the way he expected his morning to go. Maybe he should opt for Starbucks espresso to avoid this particular Jamba Juice in the future.

He narrows his eyes, gripping the strap of his gym bag even tighter now. She sees his knuckles go white. Boy's got a temper.

"Back off," he growls at her. His eyes flick down from her eyes to her mouth, noticing her pink chapped lips, but just for a second.

When his smoothie with *her* barley grass gets placed on the counter by an unassuming worker, she grabs the cup and holds it close to her chest.

He widens his eyes at the cheek of it, before his expression turns furious.

"That barley grass belongs to me," he hisses.

He grabs it back from her, their fingers grazing and spilling some of the green liquid out over the sides. She lets him have it, for now, both of them brooding as he turns on his heel and exits the Jamba Juice, slinging his gym bag over his shoulder so it bounces off his firm ass.

Maybe *she* should take up drinking espresso in the mornings. She'd be less cranky.

Callie waits at the counter for her whey protein shake, denying the impulse to chase him down, instead watching him as he walks across the street into the Cross Fit studio.

Of course, this muscular, temperamental dickhead does Cross Fit. She doesn't know what she expected.

Penn Taylor, a fellow yoga instructor at the Asana Peace and Serenity studio, had turned her on to this food subscription thing. For a set price, you could go pick up prepared foods to fit your diet. Incredibly convenient, albeit overpriced. They either delivered them to you, or you could go pick them up at a designated location for free. And Callie had been dying to try paleo for a while. It was all the yoga studio owner, Dave, a guy with an unkempt beard and a bottle of kombucha glued to his hand 24/7 talked about these days.

So Penn gave her a discount code, and she picked a designated pickup location. The delivery fee to her cottage was outrageous. Only one close to her – 47 Benhill Street – for her HIGH

OCTANE. It was convenient, especially while she was balancing her two jobs as an instructor at the yoga studio and a junior mechanic at a local auto repair shop.

It's only when she types the address into Google Maps she realizes the pickup location is *right* across the street from Asana Peace and Serenity. And she realizes she's familiar with the place already.

Callie looks through the sparkling clean windows of High Octane Cross Fit. It's empty. She knows these folks run on weird schedules with their workouts. It's a bizarre looking place, too. Rowing machines line the walls, and there are tires piled in one corner? Ropes hanging from the ceiling?

The food subscription pickup fridge is located in a corner. She tries the front door of the gym, but it's locked, so she knocks.

Cupping a hand to the glass, she peers in and sees a figure emerging from a back door, walking towards her. Ugh, it's *this* dude again. She blows a puff of air out of her cheeks, standing up straighter and squaring her shoulders.

He yanks open the door, his brow furrowed, having recognized Callie through the glass already.

"Here to steal another smoothie of mine?" he asks. He eyeballs her Asana Peace and Serenity branded crop top.

"No. I'm picking up –" she points to the fridge.

He follows her finger.

He rues the day he ever agreed to have that thing installed.

"Ugh, that was your order that came in. Fine," he lets her in, and she makes a beeline for her paleo.

"How's it going over there with my hippie uncle?" he doesn't even say it lightly, and she notices there's something there, in his tone, that indicates some tormented familial shit.

She pauses, checking for her name on the containers in the fridge and connecting the dots before answering. "Right, Dave is your uncle. Uh, he's good, always talking about that Ayurvedic stuff, but you know . . . he's around, I guess."

Despite owning the studio, Dave Dalton brooded in a back

office. His sister, Sandra, a former television personality, handled most of the studio day-to-day operations in recent years.

"Don't tell those folks I said hi," he says. It was petty of him, but he didn't care.

"I wasn't going to." she adjusts her yoga mat across her back as she struggles to balance the containers. "Do you have a bag for these or something?"

For a moment, he thinks about that. He's having some inner turmoil about *this* request as well. "I do."

"Can I have one?"

"It's in the back."

"Okay?" she shrugs. Her foot taps against the rubber flooring.

Ugh, she's needy. He ponders this again and sulks towards a door in the far back of the gym. She follows him.

"What's your name?" Callie asks, and he casts a glance over one of the massive trapezius muscles in his shoulders, surprised to find her at his heels.

"Alex Bardot."

"Right, Sandra's son," she says, her internal suspicion confirmed. There'd been talk at the studio about an Levine/Bardot family member going rogue. It was a bit of a scandal. The family was full of celebrities, but this was California. The place was crawling with celebrities.

He nods.

"I'm Callie, by the way. You're not good at conversation."

He grunts in response as he leads her into what appears to be a locker room, only it's pristine. It's the cleanest locker room she's ever seen. The lockers are stainless steel and they *shine*. He opens one with a clang and throws a tote bag at her, branded with the subscription company's logo. She catches it, and he raises his eyebrows in admiration at her catlike reflexes.

She stuffs the containers into the bag. Their eyes meet, and she looks away almost as soon as they do.

"Thanks," she says, and Callie exits the gym.

Chapter Two

She *finally* makes it to Jamba Juice one morning the following week while they still have barley grass in stock. He's blissfully nowhere to be found.

The rest of the day, though, it feels like there's something missing.

"And, just let yourself be, wherever you are..." Penn's voice is calm, and she lifts her head and lets her eyes drift over the instructor's butt, tight in black spandex. Too bad the dude was dating her roommate, Dean. She'd climb that like a tree.

"Come up into utkatasana, remember to reach up with the crown of your head..." Callie follows suit, trying to breathe in through her nose, out through her mouth.

Speaking of climbing trees, an image flashes across her mind's eye, the memory of a biceps flexing under a grey cotton jersey muscle tee, but she shakes the thought away.

Breathe in through the nose, out through the mouth. She gets lost in thought as she flows into the downward dog, all the blood rushing to her head.

Moments like these are when she's forced to sit in the reality of her existence. But, since moving to California, practicing yoga is what's grounded her through everything.

Callie grew up an orphan somewhere north of Santa Fe. She'd been homeless for a good chunk of her life. She slept in abandoned cars for most of her adolescence. In the middle of all that heat and sand, she would curl up in a back seat and lull herself to sleep with thoughts of what waves might sound like when they crashed on the sand.

But like everyone has a story, you know?

And when she saved up enough cash, learning to fix broken engines and scavenging for parts at a local junkyard, she had walked down to route 40 and stuck her thumb out, getting into a punch buggy with an earnest guy named Dean (Penn's boyfriend), and they drove out west together, to the coast and to the waves, and the rest, as they say, was history.

Speaking of stories. She always felt like hers is *just* about to start. Always on the precipice. Nothing ever felt like quite enough.

After class, Callie walks by the Cross Fit gym one day and watches Alex Bardot through the glass windows. She watches the sheer exertion as he lifts himself, over and over, into a pull-up, lifting his chin above a bar mounted to the wall, before dropping and doing a series of burpees.

She's mesmerized. He's shirtless, and his muscles strain, his body covered in a sheen of sweat, and he's so intense, it reminds her of the focus she gets during vinyasa . . . a sort of blissed-out existence.

She realizes she's gone into a bit of a daydream, watching him.

She also realizes that he's stood, grabbing a towel from a nearby chair, and is watching her right back. Her cheeks flush, and she shakes her head, tearing her gaze from his, walking away from the gym as she sips at her cold brew.

Callie especially enjoys it when guest instructors come to teach. It's a pleasant break in routine and gives her a chance to learn new techniques and teaching styles to incorporate into her own classes.

Today, a woman named Alissa Bhat is there to guide them. At the end of their session, in a corpse pose, when Callie's eyes close and she's back to thinking about the desert and heat and sand. Maybe she could go back. Maybe she *should* go back, she's spent too much time out here, on the coast, by the water, what if *they* come back to find her in Santa Fe and she's not there–but then Alissa's voice drifts to her from the front of the room –

"It's important to remember, the belonging we seek is not always behind us. It may be ahead of us, or even just around the corner." the woman's voice is soothing, palms rested upward on her knees as she sits in sukhasana.

This statement jars Callie from her train of thought, and she feels tears prickle at the corner of her eyes, and almost as if Alissa senses this sudden discomfort from one of her students –

"Wherever you are today, be all there. Your body is trying to tell you something. Let it out, and sit in the feeling," Alissa tells the class. With this comfort, Callie allows the tears to stream down her cheeks, breathing through it.

When the class ended, Callie rolls her mat up, strapping it to her back and giving a heartfelt *"Thank you,"* to Alissa as she departs.

She stops at the check-in desk, studying the schedule for the upcoming week. Sandra has been growing the number of classes Callie teaches, now that she's had more training under her belt. It's becoming tougher to balance with the auto repair gig. But she does a little happy dance when she notices she's been scheduled for a prime time yoga session that Sunday–the 10:00 a.m. spot, always booked full of eager young women who like to hit the studio before brunch.

Lucky for her. She heads over to the juice place for a pick me up.

They're standing by the Jamba Juice pickup counter. A kerfuffle avoided this morning, with enough barley grass in stock for them both.

"Why Cross Fit?"

"Why yoga?"

"Fair."

"I don't know. I . . . we all need an outlet."

"So, mine is candles and meditation. Yours is..." she gestures with her palm.

"Pushing my body and stamina to extreme limits and constantly testing myself, yes."

"It just seems so brutal."

"You're so right," is his reply, and for the first time, she sees a small, genuine smile play at the corner of his lips. He pauses. "It's not that I don't believe in what my uncle and mother do, you know," Alex shifts on the balls of his feet. He hates bringing up family.

"Oh?"

"It's just . . . different. Everyone's different, Callie. And the lessons they have to teach over there, across the street? It's not that I don't know them, or haven't tried. But everyone's different."

He remembered her name. She takes a moment to ponder this before nodding. "I just couldn't ever imagine finding peace on a rowing machine."

"I can't find peace folded over like a pretzel accompanied by candlelight. My thoughts get so loud–" He stops himself there.

She wants to tell him to continue, but she barely knows him. Well, she knows enough. But her perception of him is shifting in front of her. He's no longer this untouchable enigma with an uncanny ability to fuck up her smoothie orders. A whole person is coming to life in front of her, complete with both sharp edges and rounded corners and a fire burning right beneath the surface.

They go their separate ways after receiving their orders, but a couple hours later, Callie waits outside the door of the locked

Cross Fit gym, swiping on Tinder while she waits for Alex to come let her in so she can fetch this week's paleo.

Funnily enough, *"Alex, 29"* pops up on her screen. The location algorithms on these apps are *scarily* accurate. What a terrible profile picture.

She glares up at him when he yanks open the door to stare down at her in annoyance.

"Why don't you just get this shit delivered to you?"

She holds her phone up to him, his profile open on her iPhone screen. She makes a show of swiping left with her thumb. He narrows his eyes as she pockets her phone.

"Get a new profile picture. You look like a fuckboy."

She nudges past him, elbowing his abdomen as she does so and hits him with her yoga mat.

As Callie opens the fridge and stocks her bag with her subscription boxes, she realizes he's set up shop against the wall next to the fridge, leaning back with his arms crossed over his chest.

"I swiped right," he tells her. Is he *forlorn?* Is this a joke?

She laughs and wants to say something snarky and dismiss him, but a thought dawns on her.

You know, she has needs of her own.

"Did you really?"

He shrugs. "I liked your dimples." He's being honest.

She smiles, the gears turning in her head. "Which ones?"

Callie sets her tote bag on the ground, closes the fridge door, and turns to give him a view of her butt in yoga pants, before lifting the back of her tank top up, revealing the two well-defined indentations right above her ass. They don't call them dimples of Venus for nothing.

He swallows. His throat feels thick. "I–"

"Is anyone else here?" He shakes his head in response. "What, do you like, own the place?" He nods. Thank god.

She bends over, making a show of it, to pick up her tote bag and shove the food back in the fridge. She drops her yoga mat to the floor, and walks back towards that locker room Alex had taken her to the other week, during her first visit, casting a look over her shoulder and jerking her head as a sign for him to follow her.

He does.

Chapter Three

When they get to the locker room, she tugs her tank top off, revealing a dark mesh sports bra. She turns to face him. He's leaning in the doorway. If this were a cartoon, his jaw would be on the floor.

He can see the outline of her nipples through the mesh. Holy shit.

"Don't you have somewhere to be? Go stand on your head, or something?" he asks before pressing his lips together. He's not trying to contain the saliva pooling at the back of his mouth.

"Shut up," she snarls at him, walking towards him and stepping on her toes before latching his lower lip between her teeth. "You're going to make up for every morning of mine you've ruined."

He supposes he can agree.

Callie yanks off his muscle tee without ceremony, revealing some of the most defined pecs and abdominals she's ever seen. She finds she wants her tongue on his muscles, like yesterday.

"Fuck," he groans as she does that. God, he tastes a bit like sweat and salt, but she loves it in this soft, familiar, weird way, and she pushes that thought way back deep down into a dark corner of herself, because let's not fucking go there, maybe? This encounter is about a release of tension. That's it.

"Can you lift?" she chides him, straightening as she releases one of his nipples from her lips. He grins, as this is his domain.

He lifts her like she's *nothing*. His hands hook under her thighs and he lifts her lithe body up so that her legs hook around his waist, and he holds her there with one arm while the other undoes her ponytail and grasps her neck. Her skin and hair are so soft.

Her own hands travel to the back of his head to latch onto his hair, wet from what appears to be a recent shower, as she gets a vague whiff of his soap, a scent that fills her with that warmth again. She bites his earlobe in response to this. He gasps a bit before pressing their lips together.

And, it's clumsy at first. His lips are *super* plump and soft and he tastes kind of like cough drops. They're both a bit out of breath from the excitement. Their tongues glide together, and it's like he's trying to Jiffy Lube her tonsils or something. He gets so enthusiastic. It reminds them both of all the best, most exciting parts of what it was once like to be a teenager.

He likes how warm she is, here in his arms.

And they're both still far too dressed. He's still got on his mesh shorts, she's still in a sports bra and cropped yoga pants.

Alex drops her to the floor, and she lets out a surprised gasp as he does so. He gets to his knees and begins tugging her crops and her sports undies down. Callie kicks off her socks and white Stan Smith sneakers.

On his knees, he looks up at her through thick lashes, an idea forming on his face.

"How flexible are you?" he asks. She smiles down at him. *Her* domain.

Having just finished Bikram, her muscles are still pretty nice and warm and pliant.

She turns to face away from him, and he only has a moment to enjoy the view of her perky, freckled round ass and those dimples of Venus as she bends over before she's lifting her right leg into a standing split, her body doubled over as one leg extends far above her head in a straight line.

Her leg muffles her voice as she tells him, "Urdhva Prasarita Eka Padasana." Her voice is steady, and he can see her grinning against her calf from this position.

The thing is, in this position, with the lower half of her body unclothed, the view is obscene. She's not bare, but she does some sort of landscaping. Her bikini line is a perfect triangle of curly hair.

And he can see everything. The way she's stretched in front of where he kneels, he can *smell* the perfect pink glistening folds of her aching pussy. His stomach knots itself into a pang of absolute *want*.

Fuck. Holy shit. Fuck.

"Can I eat you out like this?" he asks, not sure where it's coming from, but she is calling to him like a siren and he's a sailor on the high seas.

From behind her left leg, she adjusts her face to meet his gaze, upside down, and she nods.

He stabilizes her pose with a hand around her waist, the other snaking up to grip the thigh that's stretched into the air, and he presses small bites into her smooth skin, relishing the salty taste there, and he realizes she's shaking a bit.

"You–you okay?" he asks one of her thighs.

"If you don't fucking put that tongue where it belongs, I'm coming up there and smothering your face myself," she tells him, her voice sounding strained, though not from the exertion of the pose.

He brings his mouth to her to find her *critically* wet, her arousal evident around the dark pink skin there, and decides to make a meal out of her. Wasting no time, he licks her from clit to slit–oh god, it's all upside down in this position–his hands stabilizing her as he plunges his tongue deep into her and tongue-fucks her into an alternate dimension.

She swears she's ascending. Callie's being held there only by the one foot she has on the ground and by Alex's hands at her waist. The combined endorphins of holding the pose and the sensation of getting filled like this is sending her to another level of being. Talk about being mindful. An asteroid could be headed for Earth right now. Would she care?

"Oh my *god*, Callie, you taste so fucking good," he pulls away from her, and she swears she feels tears at the corners of her eyes. There's a whimper at the back of her throat from the sudden lack of contact, but what's more jarring is the slow burn in her right leg now, bordering on impossible. She's reaching her limit with this pose.

"I–I'm not sure I–I can't–" she says, but before she can finish, Callie feels Alex begin to untwist her, bringing her right leg down from its split so she's bent over in a forward fold. The stretch still feels incredible, and it alleviated some of the tension this way.

He leans forward and sucks on her exposed clit again, but with a languid tempo. And then, he reaches a hand up to fill her with one thick finger, like a knife into hot butter.

"Oh my god, Callie, you're so tight, you're so *fucking* tight, how many fingers can I fit in here, fuck," he murmurs against her pussy.

The vibrations of his voice against her folds cause her to shiver. She also didn't expect him to talk this dirty. She's into it.

After fucking her with one, he adds a second long, broad finger. At this angle, bent over, he's able to reach deep within her, at an angle she's never able to reach on her own, and she feels full and stimulated.

Her quads shake from exertion and an impending climax, heat building in her hips and abdomen while he sucks at her clit at an agonizingly slow pace and finger fucks her.

She gasps against her shins, dancing at the edge of her orgasm, sparks behind her eyelids.

"Oh my god, I'm going to–"

He pulls away from her, breaking all contact.

Callie's eyes fly wide open, and she widens her stance a bit to look up at him through her legs. He's smiling at her like a loon, and all her focus goes to her aching core, where cool air is now hitting it instead of his merciless tongue.

"What. The. *Fuck*," she snarls.

"I want your thighs around my head when you come all over my face," he tells her, reaching around to lift her up and lay her down across a bench located near the row of lockers.

Callie holds herself steady by gripping the area of the bench up around her head, and Alex shuffles over to bring his mouth *back to where it belongs.*

She obliges his request, pressing her thighs to either side of his head–oh, his ears are kind of big, that's cute. Wait, shut up–to hold him there in a vice-like grip.

"Finish what you started," she tells him before bringing one hand down to pull that head of curly hair closer to the apex of her thighs and pressing his mouth to her messy cunt.

She hears him say something against her wet folds. It sounds like a swear, but her mind goes blank as he just goes for it, alternating between gloriously attentive licks and sucking on her clit. He alternates the pressure a bit here and there, he's so unpredictable, and her hips twitch of their own accord as she's brought close to orgasm, only to be left dangling at the precipice when he moves away from her clit and thrusts his tongue into her.

"Fucking *hell*," she whimpers, a sound she didn't know she had in her, high and whiny, and Alex snakes one hand up around her to press down on her abdomen and hold her still.

His other hand finds its way between her legs to replace his tongue with his fingers, and he's fucking her with them now, curling up into that patch of nerves in her pussy that makes her writhe a bit on the wooden bench. She palms her tits through the mesh fabric of her sports bra, desperate for friction on her nipples, for something, for anything.

Oh my god. Alex's tongue finds her clit just as he presses once, twice, three times up into that spot, and a dam breaks, flowing out of her and covering his chin.

And the tactician that he is, he stays with her through it, his fingers coaxing out every drop, his lips pressed around her clit while she comes for a solid, hell, *at least*, forty-five seconds, he's been holding her at the edge for so long.

Her thighs turn to putty and she drops her legs wide to the floor. She looks down at him through her haze, with heavy-lidded eyes, and he's scooping her up and bringing her down to the floor with him so that he can sit up against the lockers, pulling her between his legs and cradling her.

It's gentle of him, and she nuzzles into the crook of his neck beneath his chin in her post-orgasm bliss.

Blame it on those pesky endorphins.

"I'd like to fuck you now," he murmurs into her hair bun.

She hums against the skin at his throat in agreement, but neither of them moves just yet.

It's like they've both got all the time in the world.

Chapter Four

"I'd like to fuck you now."

Alex gets up off the ground, picking her up bridal style as he does so, exerting himself.

There's a tall pile of red gym mats in the locker's corner room, and he sets her down here, allowing her legs to dangle off the edge. At this height, his hips align with hers. How convenient.

Now that she's had a moment to allow herself some time to zone out post-orgasm, she realizes that there's an ache back between her legs. It's not that the foreplay wasn't enough. It's just that she can now see the outline of his hard-on through the mesh of his shorts and, like, she knows she's going to be missing out if she runs for the Los Padres hills right now.

Would not be the first time she ghosted on a dude after he ate her out.

Callie is a busy girl, after all.

But no, he's got a long, hard treat for her under those Adidas shorts.

She's long overdue for this.

He eyes her thighs, spread wide on the mats, and the glistening mess she's made across her freckled skin. Fuck. At least these mats are easy to clean, because they're about to get a lot stickier..

"How deep do you want it?" he asks, tugging his shorts down so his cock bounces free. He runs his hand along the length of it. He's been hard and leaking since she bent over at the fridge in her yoga pants earlier.

"Fuck. I want to feel you between my eyeballs," she whispers in response, spreading her thighs even wider.

He leans forward, feeling her with his free hand, making sure she's more than ready to take him.

Mission is a go.

"Wait - uh - are we - we good?"

She points to her left arm, where there's a slight indentation indicating one of those birth control implants. He nods in understanding.

"Are you, you know –" she asks, realizing they've both got a few hoeish tendencies, but hoping they both have the general common sense and wherewithal to get tested.

"Oh, yeah, uh, good there too," he mumbles a bit. He uses his hand to line himself up to her entrance.

"Oh my god, I do not know how you're going to fit, but do it already," she squirms a little at the sensation of him spreading her open with just the tip of his cock.

"Trust me, babe, I'm planning on fucking you from here into the next star system," as he slides smoothly into home base with one satisfying thrust.

Fuck. She must do kegels.

"Star system?" she gasps. She hasn't felt this full in years. He's got one of those magical dicks that's both long and like girthy? Which never happens. It's usually one or the other, and how is this dude still single?

"I was a Carl Sagan fan. Forget it," Alex grunts in response, hoping he can just fuck that thought right out of her.

This chick doesn't need to know about his childhood infatuation with Jodie Foster in *Contact*. It's embarrassing.

To distract her from this momentary lapse in his hard outer shell, he leans down to grab her ankles and lift her legs high into the air, holding them parallel to his chest.

He's in so deep. She goes to grasp at something, anything–oh, the edge of the mat will work–but he's like, fucking her so hard she's kind of backing up against the wall now, and her head is sort of hitting the brick, so she motions for him to chill.

"You're going to give me a concussion. Flip me over," she orders. He obliges, turning her onto her chest and running a grateful hand flat over those lower back dimples of hers. She's bending over the mats now, with much better balance.

He has an idea and slides back into her. She's so smooth and wet and velvety. He's practicing a lot of self control right now. He deserves a medal maybe.

"Holy fuck, want to feel you come on my cock," he grunts, reaching forward a bit to grab her hair in its bun and use it to gain leverage as he fucks into her.

She didn't realize she was into getting her hair pulled until the exact moment he did it, and now she's wondering why she'd ever denied herself this experience. The slight pain is really quite delicious. He's not pulling so hard that it's uncomfortable, but just enough, and she whimpers a bit, the two of them tugging in a perfect balance.

"God, yes, pull my hair," she groans, and he grips even more of her brown locks. She finds that the feel of his massive hands on the back of her head fills her with a weird sense of familiarity and calm that she just wants to lean into. It should have been an impersonal, rough gesture–hair pulling–but it's the opposite.

Alex leans over her then, covering her back with his broad chest, intensifying the sensation of skin on skin. It's electrifying.

He lets go of her hair and circles his hand around to grasp her neck, his calloused fingers against her smooth throat. His other hand travels down between her legs to circle her clit, before he increases the tempo and friction in harmony with his dick.

There's something about this position, with a hand around

her neck, another between her legs, his dick hitting that spot up near her cervix (NOT her actual cervix, to be clear, *dear god* go Google the anterior fornix), that deep dicking feeling she ever gets to enjoy. It makes her feel stuffed and stretched and *complete*.

Oh god.

"Fuck," she whimpers, his hand gentle against her throat.

"That's right," he murmurs into the sensitive space at the nape. It tickles her a bit, but she loves it.

"Fuck," she's mumbling again, incoherent.

"Mhmm," he sucks a spot into her skin. She hopes it leaves a mark.

She goes from about 60 to 100 in milliseconds, the sensation of his lips at the back of her neck and his satisfying attention to her clit doing her in.

It's this weird breaking point, where she knows she's coming, but then there's something else, right behind the corner, and his dick is hitting it, and she's there, right THERE, clenching around him, and she goes from orgasm to a blissful euphoria and he holds her there as her eyes fly open, a choked cry coming from the back of her throat as she clenches down around his cock, hard.

"That's what I was talking about," he whispers.

She thought she had known bliss after he ate her out. No. That was like tapas. This was a full five-course buffet meal with an endless dessert cart and maybe a few dessert cocktails on the side.

She's still pretty muddled, but she mumbles something like "Inside me. Come inside," and he thinks he's got it all under control until that point, because he too loses it when he hears her say *that* and comes right into her.

God, Callie loves getting rawed. She can't feel her legs.

"Are we even?" he asks with a small, playful smile.

She's forgotten her own name. "Even? For what?"

"The barley grass."

"Fuck the barley grass," she mumbles, throwing an elbow across her face. She'd rather like to nap here, on this pile of mats, for maybe the next century.

"I'd rather it be you," he answers, and she swears if he had sent that as a text there would have been a weird wink face emoji attached to it.

Realizing she doesn't know the time and has to get to the garage for her shift, she sits upright.

She's also just fucked her boss' son. She hadn't thought about it from that perspective. Oh my god, she has to get out of there.

"Can you hand me–" she points to the discarded cropped yoga pants and underwear lying on the floor. He obliges before pulling his shorts back up around his hips. He has *such* a nice iliac furrow. She hadn't had time to appreciate that musculature earlier.

She realizes her sports bra had stayed on this whole time. Maybe there could be a part two where it comes off? She dresses her lower half.

Alex brings over her shoes and socks as well and watches her.

"This was fun," she tells him.

"Can I get your number?" he asks. He sort of looks and sounds like she has hit him over the head with a baseball bat.

"No, but I can get yours." Callie realizes she left her phone out with her bag near the fridge at the front of the gym. Great, now she has to walk of shame out there. With the rowing machines and everything.

He follows her, and they're not talking now, which is weird, because that was the most talking she's ever done during a hookup. She's used to silence and muffled grunting.

What in the hell is she doing?

She pulls her phone out and waits for him to tell her his number. No thank you, she doesn't want him to call her. So, she can enter his contact info herself, storing those digits away for when she's thirsty later. Which may or may not happen.

His face falls a bit at the realization that he's helpless here, dependent on her and her desire to text him. He tells her his number, and she enters it as "Cross Fit, Rock Hard Abs."

Callie grabs her paleo from the fridge, swings her yoga mat over her shoulder, and gives him a quick once-over.

"Yeah, thanks," she tells him. "I've got to get to my other job, but this was a blast."

He doesn't respond, but leans up against the fridge in that pouty way of his, and watches her leave.

That ass in yoga pants will be the death of him.

Chapter Five

She makes it to the garage just in time for her shift.

Callie does love her second job as an auto mechanic. She likes working with her hands. It's a delightful change of pace from the vibes at the yoga studio. And the owner of the garage is this gorgeous woman with bright hair, Ashley Haven. She and Sandra are friends. They do Margarita Mondays together. It's how Callie got this second gig.

"I would like to improve our marketing. Can you help, Callie?" Ashley is pleading with her as Callie bends over the engine of a vintage green Cadillac.

The woman has been on her ass about this social media marketing thing. You know, because Callie is a millennial, and knows all about digital marketing strategy because she can take a semi-blurry photo of avocado toast.

"Of course I'll help." And it's no skin off Callie's back. She can create an Instagram account for Haven and the garage, easy.

An hour later, leaning up against the Cadillac, she sets up the Instagram handle @HavenAuto and begins loading up a few images of the nicer vintage cars they'd worked on.

When she clicks back to the main Instagram feed, one of the

first "suggested follows" is an account by the name of @AXGRAY.

Huh?

They advertise the account as GET SHREDDED WITH AX.

This has nothing to do with auto repairs. Why is it showing up on this feed?

She clicks through to the page out of curiosity and feels laughter choke out of the back of her throat.

Oh, my god.

Ax Gray. GET SHREDDED. GET RIPPED. SIXTY DAY CROSS FIT TOTAL BODY CHALLENGE. COME TO HIGH OCTANE FITNESS TODAY. *(mgmt: stanley@high-octane.net)*

Oh, my god. He has a fitspo alter ego on Instagram.

She realizes this fiasco may have something to do with the fact that she signed up for the auto shop Instagram account with *her* personal phone number (Callie doesn't have an Insta of her own), and the app had prompted her to connect her address book. Oh that, that made more sense now.

There are so many ridiculous photos of him flexing in mirrors. He has a few aesthetic photos of protein shakes, a bird's-eye view of chicken (side of broccoli), and a couple videos of him lifting. Oh, and a couple how-to videos. How philanthropic of him. "How to Get an Eight-Pack"? That's a bit of an overestimation on his end, but whatever.

It's hilarious.

It's also weirdly hot, now that he's been inside her? Like, those muscles are *objectively* nice to look at. Gives her something to remember him by. She opens a video of him climbing up a rope. Those biceps deserve her undivided attention.

But if she had seen this Instagram account a week ago? No way would she have let this dude raw her the way he just did. He looks like a total dude bro who only drinks Pabst Blue Ribbon and knows what an ice luge is. Holy shit.

She swipes out of the account, tapping softly so she doesn't like any of his posts or follow him, and swipes away the original notification prompting her to follow him. The auto repair shop does not need this stuff on their Instagram feed.

Callie heads into the office area next to the garage. She hears light laughter coming from Haven's desk space, and sees Sandra Levine, in one of her signature kaftans, leaning over the mahogany desk to curl one of Haven's tendrils of purple hair around her finger.

Callie clears her throat while making a show of loading a tool box onto a desk so they know they're not alone.

Sandra looks up, chuckling.

"My favorite vinyasa expert. Callie, how are you?" Sandra steps away from Haven's desk and approaches Callie with open arms, her colorful kaftan flowing around her a bit from the fans they have set up around the office. Callie gives her a hug.

How did this kind, free-spirited woman give birth to the guy she had fucked earlier?

"Good, just finished setting up an Instagram for us here."

"We hired someone to do ours for the studio. Her name's Kinsey. I could give you her contact info?"

Ashley smiles. "I've got this under control, Sandra. Callie knows what she's doing. Don't you, Callie?"

The fuck? Callie nods. But ugh, now she has to learn how to use apps like Snapseed or whatever. At least she can now throw "digital marketing" on her LinkedIn. Sounds legit.

———

It's been a week, and Callie still hasn't texted him. She figures she'll run into him at some point.

"Hey Ax," she says, coming up behind him in line at Jamba.

He turns dramatically to face her. His face is expressionless.

"How did–"

"I have a cell phone."

"But–"

"It's the 21st century and nowhere is safe, buddy. By the way, an eight-pack is a bit of a stretch. Who drinks Soylent?"

"It's a contract."

"Fascinating."

Alex furrows his brow and huffs. He spins on his heel to face the counter. "I'd like to order all your remaining barley grass shots for the day, please."

The cashier looks at him, bored. "We don't have a set quantity to, uh, track remaining stock?"

"Don't you have a bucket? A bowl somewhere?"

"It's like a plant. We cut the barley grass fresh -"

"So give me the damn potted plant, then."

Callie raises her eyebrows. She takes out her phone while he throws this little tantrum of his and swipes through Tinder, making it super obvious that she's swiping right on most of these folks.

He glances back at her and notices her swiping habits, because she sees the tips of his ears go kind of red.

"Oh yeah, she's cute," Callie offers commentary, holding up the profile of a gorgeous, tall, muscular woman with blue eyes and short platinum blonde hair. Alex narrows his eyes as she swipes right. He storms over to the pickup counter, where they've assembled a literal *carton of potted barley grass*.

Callie swipes right on the woman. "A match!" She approaches the cashier to place her order. "Just uh, your energy booster for now, I guess. Since the barley grass is gone."

She walks over to join him at the pickup counter. He's struggling to balance both the barley grass and his gym bag. She holds up her phone screen to him, Tinder still open.

"Oh, I love me a ginger," she makes another show of swiping right on *Leon*, a pale serious looking brunette. He's someone she would never have swiped right on in any other situation, ever. But she's making a point. "Oh, look Ax, he's another match!"

He grunts, hobbling out of the Jamba Juice with a scowl on his face. She follows him, forgetting her smoothie. Whoops.

She hovers near him as they wait at the curb for the light to change. He leans over to sniff his barley grass, wrinkling his nose.

"Do you have a juicer or something?" she asks, like this is the most normal thing in the world.

"What? No."

"How are you going to make the barley grass shots?"

"I don't–I'll just eat it–" he bends down and takes a bite from the blades of grass.

She stares at him, open-mouthed and wide-eyed. This is some next-level drama queen shit. Time for her to nope the fuck out of here.

"So anyway, I'm — I'll just text you when I'm ready to get shredded with Ax Gray."

He scowls at her, barley grass sticking out of his mouth. It's almost endearing.

"You look like a donkey."

Alex growls, spitting out the greenery. He drops his gym bag to the ground, places the carton on top of it, and turns back to face her. She imagines steam coming out of his big ears. Callie looks up at him, fluttering her eyelashes a bit.

He tackles her, leaning down so that he can throw her over his shoulder and move her back towards one of the brick walls of the Jamba Juice establishment.

He hoists her up against the wall, his hands tight around her trim waist, her yoga mat providing padding between her back and the bricks.

"We're in public," Callie tells him.

He leans in, close, so fucking close, and presses his plush lips to her throat. The touch is so light in comparison to his heat and aggression just moments before.

Callie's a sucker. She's never been able to handle the neck thing. The minute anyone gets their lips near that area? She's done for. So, in full view of sidewalk passerby, she's letting this dude neck her, and she's letting out a little gasp in the process, and she feels *heat* pool between her thighs, and then he's dropping her to the ground–not hard enough to hurt, but hard enough to startle her.

He goes back over to his barley grass and gym bag, leaving her panting up against the brick wall as he stumbles over to his gym.

Thank god she has a Hitachi at home, am I right?

Chapter Six

Callie is bent over backward in kapotasana, trying to breathe into the stretch, when she finds herself distracted by muffled thumping noises.

She has a soft Spotify playlist going on the speakers, but it's got nothing on the groans reverberating through the walls of the stucco cottage she shares with her roommate, Dean.

Honestly, it's not even that she *wants* to live alone. She's done enough of that. She appreciates the creature comfort that comes with a (usually) quiet roommate. But at times like these . . .

Don't get her wrong, Dean is awesome. It's not that. He's earnest and genuine. Maybe clingy at times. He's got a great smile. Sometimes he's a little confused and misguided, but his heart's always in the right place. *And* he's the guy who got her out of that desert with his little punch buggy, so she'll always be grateful for that. She never thought she'd ever have a close friend like him.

She just, only slightly regrets introducing him to her coworker, Penn Taylor. Those two now look at each other like the goddamn sun rises in the other's eyes.

It's cute, but it makes her jealous and reminds her she's got as many issues as Vogue, and will never have a healthy, functioning relationship in her life. She's a formerly homeless orphan with a slew of trust issues and an empty void inside of her the size of a black hole. Callie's got a good head on her shoulders, but like, maybe she'd benefit from some therapy.

Too bad Congress doesn't care about improving a failing healthcare system.

Any way. She also knows for a fact that Dean and Penn have the nastiest, loudest sex she's ever heard. Not that she's overheard a lot of sex? Growing up, the way she did? But she gets the idea Penn's exceptional flexibility and ability to do a tittibhasana absolutely blows Dean away.

She doesn't get the idea; she hears it. Loudly. The sound of Bon Iver strumming on her Spotify has nothing on the muffled thwacks of Dean's headboard hitting the wall.

She sighs, and comes up out of her own pose, deciding she might head over to Haven's and check out a gorgeous blue and white striped vintage Shelby GT350 that had appeared in the repair garage the other day. She wanted dibs before the other mechanic, Rita McKinnon, got her hands on it.

"Who left that here?" Callie jerks her thumb out towards the GT350 in the garage as she enters Haven's office area. She adjusts her beige utility jumpsuit, rolling the sleeves up around her elbows and fiddling with the embroidered name tag.

Haven glances up from her brick of a computer. She is in a gorgeous lavender blouse, accessorized with dangly silver earrings. She's not someone you would ever expect to own an auto repair shop, but here we are. Callie is in awe of her. Haven is a successful local businesswoman, thriving and taking advantage of the rich local interest in vintage automobiles.

"Dave," is Haven's casual response, looking back down at the QuickBooks open on her screen.

"Wait. *Dave* Dave? Sandra's brother? You're kidding me."

Haven narrows her eyes at Callie's language. "No cursing. He doesn't want it anymore."

"You're joking. It's a classic," Callie remarks, astonished.

Haven shrugs before tucking some of her hair back into a

silver headband. "He wants us to sell it, give it away. I don't think he cares."

"And Sandra is okay with this?" Callie tilts her head.

Haven blinks, her gaze still fixed on the computer screen in front of her. "You've got a lot to learn about that family."

A few hours later, after she's sized up the engine on the Shelby and finished repairing a Camaro, Callie ventures back into the office to grill Haven. The lady doesn't just get to make offhanded comments about the Daltons and not spill the goddamn tea.

"Can you tell me about Alex?" Callie asks, stopping by the water cooler in the office to fill up her canteen.

"Alex?"

"Sandra's son. It's just that his gym is across the street from Sandra's studio, and he never comes over." Let Haven think she's just fishing for family drama and dirt.

"Oh. He was such a good kid." Haven looks away from her computer for a moment, out the window. "I mean, he could be trouble, you know? He was a boy," they share a knowing glance, both their eyebrows lifting towards their hairlines in unison. "And so much like his father." Haven gives an eye roll at this.

"Right, Max."

"Max, as you know, is a bit of a legend himself. He won the Daytona 500 once, you know."

Callie was aware. Racing had been big, back where she was from. She'd tried her hand at it a few times. She'd even had a few gigs at a local track, working on crash repairs.

Haven was downplaying Max's feats. Callie had seen him once. He'd done a publicity stunt down at the Sandia Speedway when she was younger, maybe eight years old, and she roguishly climbed the bleachers without buying a ticket. She could remember the feel of hot metal against her palms, sand blowing into her face as she struggled to catch a peek of the famous Red Razor and its hotshot driver, Max Bardot. What a legend.

She also knew the guy had fallen from fame in recent years, and she hadn't heard about him in a decade.

When she had first realized Alex's parentage, she had already become too familiar with Sandra and Dave to truly be star struck by the connection. They were her bosses now. And it's not like she had ever met Max, anyway. He spent a lot of time divided between Vegas and the local penitentiary.

"So they're not close? Alex and his dad?"

Haven guffaws at this. She kicks back in her rolling office chair, chuckling to herself before standing and watering a few of the succulents and ferns she keeps littered around her desk.

Callie takes that as a firm *fuck* no (tormented familial shit, confirmed), and decides she might as well get back to work. She ventures out into the garage to eyeball the gorgeous white GT350, complete with blue stripes.

Haven follows her and leans in the garage's doorway. "Speaking of the Daltons, I think that car was his mother's."

"His mother?"

Haven looks to Callie, surprised. "You know who Dave's mother was, right?"

"No?" Callie wipes some sweat off her forehead as she shakes her head.

Haven grins. "Gorgeous. Incredible. Actual royalty, you know. She was an *actual* princess."

Callie is stunned, but not surprised, at this point. Now that she'd made the move to California, she ran into bougie folks constantly. They frequented the yoga studio, too. "I did not know."

"Well, you know how royal bloodlines can get these days. It was some defunct house, some European bloodline, anyway. They're pretty irrelevant now. Even so, fascinating. She married that fellow from that one movie, the big movie star? Oh, what was his name? He was in all the black and white films, even before my time..."

Callie fiddles with a wrench on her tool bench. "Hold the fuck up. That means, technically, Dave and Sandra are..."

Haven narrows her eyes again at Callie's curse. "Language. A prince and princess, sure. If you want to get technical. But, again, it's not like they're getting invited to the Queen's royal garden party. No money attached to the name, or anything. Dave's father spent it all in the eighties. Just one of those fun little life facts." Haven waves her hand with a smile.

Callie doesn't say it out loud, but the realization dawns on her she had fucked a prince.

The more you know. This is what she got for living under a literal rock for two decades. She grew up without Wi-Fi, and had only gotten her hands on a working smart phone about two years ago.

She idly wondered what Prince Bardot was up to. Callie hadn't texted him, which in the twenty-first-century dating world equated to two centuries.

If she would not text him, Alex thought, he didn't care. Who cared? He didn't. Alex tapped that ass. He could move on with his life now.

The Jamba Juice was something he could avoid. Never go there. Ever again.

This is what he told himself as he bent over in pain, having lost count of his burpees.

His business partner, Leon Baxter (he would never forgive Callie for swiping right on this dude, even if she didn't know who she was even swiping on), chuckles with a sneer as he passes by with a stack of folders. "Careful, Gray. Don't tire yourself."

Alex has half a mind to tackle the dude to the ground, maybe throw him across the gym like a Frisbee or something, but refrains for now. He pants, his hands resting on his knees as he catches his breath. "Are those for me?" He nods towards the folders.

"Stanley sent them over. Contracts for you to review. Sign them. Give them back to me." Baxter's voice drips with contempt.

Alex supposes he doesn't have a choice. "Just leave them on my desk in the back. I'll get to them after this."

Baxter smoothes his gel-slicked hair back and stalks off towards their shared office.

Alex saunters over to one of the rowing machines and settles in, swallowing some bile that had crawled its way up the back of his throat. He begins, letting his mind drift away as his body settles into a steady, familiar, unrelenting pace.

It's just that she smelled fantastic. Salt and sandalwood. Of course, she'd been a decent lay.

He speeds up his movements on the machine, shaking the thought away with a jerk of his head.

Why did she have to work for his mother? Things might be easier if she didn't.

He groans now, his muscles shaking from the exertion and sheen of sweat collecting on his forehead and biceps.

Frustration growing, he jumps off the machine, walking around it in a rage-filled pace, flexing his arms with a borderline feral growl. He didn't want to sign any more contracts or pose for any more dumb photo shoots where they covered him with oil.

He notices Baxter standing in the gym's doorway office, sneering at the sight of Alex losing his temper like this. It's a common occurrence. In fact, Alex bet that if Stanley didn't have the two of them in a binding chokehold, Baxter would be off running his own venture. Alex would be *glad* to be rid of this red-headed rat.

Alex yells across the gym, spit flying from his mouth, "I could have you for dinner, bro!"

At that, Baxter scampers back into the office to hide, because the ginger knows it's true.

Chapter Seven

Here's the thing. Callie is a red-blooded American female. Well, sort of. There's that strange accent of hers and the question of her true parentage. So, naturally, she's been thinking about this whole prince thing for a solid week. Who *isn't* into those fairytale vibes? While avoiding buying smoothies. After all, it's far more economical to make them at home.

It's way past 11:00 pm, and so far today she's taught three yoga classes and she's now finishing a shift at Haven's.

Callie wipes her palm across her forehead, smearing a bit of grease across it in the process. She pulls the top half of her jumpsuit down around her waist, revealing a white tank top beneath, and walks over to her designated work area.

She's in desperate need of some R&R.

Her iPhone tempts her from where it charges at the corner of her workbench, perched atop a red toolbox.

She thinks about her next move for three seconds before grabbing the phone and opening up his contact screen.

Her fingers pause over the keyboard as she hits "message."

Callie: *you up?*
Cross Fit, Rock Hard Abs: *new phone, who's this?*
Callie: *u didn't even have my number in the first place*

Cross Fit, Rock Hard Abs: *I really did break my phone. dropped it*

Alex Bardot had not, in fact, dropped his phone. He had thrown it. Across his apartment, only last week. He's gone through four phones this year alone.

Callie: *sucks*
Cross Fit, Rock Hard Abs: *who is this*
Callie: *you've got three guesses, your highness*
Cross Fit, Rock Hard Abs: *I'll kill you man*
Callie: *no.*
Cross Fit, Rock Hard Abs: *ok I'm not playing this game whoever this is. blocking you, good night*

Callie's eyes glaze over and she thinks about her Hitachi plugged in at the foot of her bed back home. She supposes she doesn't *have* to make her next move . . . screw it.

Callie: *[IMAGE SENT]*

There's like, a solid five minutes here where she thinks he's blocked her and it hasn't gone through, but then –

Cross Fit, Rock Hard Abs: *oh hey, what's up?*

Smooth.

Callie: *it's awful cold tonight*
Cross Fit, Rock Hard Abs: *it's 80 degrees out*
Callie: *dude*
Cross Fit, Rock Hard Abs: *what?*
Callie: *come over*
Cross Fit, Rock Hard Abs: *you ghosted me*
Callie: *I did no such thing.*
Cross Fit, Rock Hard Abs: *[ghost emoji]*
Callie: *come over, and I promise to suck your soul out through your dick*
Callie: *[CURRENT LOCATION SENT]*

It's not fifteen minutes before she hears a shuffling from outside the garage.

"Uh, hello?"

He's wandering around out front, a confused look on his face. She slinks out the garage door, twirling a wrench in her hand.

"Hey there, your majesty."

He's surprised to see her there, outside a dimly lit garage, illuminated by flickering fluorescent lights. He thought she was summoning him to her apartment or something. Like a normal person would.

"Yeah. Who told you about that?"

"Haven. Your mom's friend. I work for her." Callie points to the signage above their heads.

"You're also an auto mechanic?" He raises his eyebrows a bit. He's impressed. She's still got a few surprises up her sleeve.

It also dawns on him she *booty called* him to her *place of employment*.

"Didn't you know that?"

"You never mentioned. And I searched for you on Facebook, I couldn't find anything."

"I'm only on LinkedIn," is her response. She smirks a bit at the realization that he tried to find her online.

"You're not on any other social media?"

She shakes her head, but steps back from the garage stoop and motions for him to join her inside. He hesitates, but follows her, his red and black Adidas slides smacking on the concrete floor. Callie hits the garage door switch so that it rumbles closed behind them.

"I don't know. I never saw the point. Sometimes I think it'd be useful, you know, for the yoga thing? Expand there a bit? But."

"I could teach you," he says, like he's eager to pass on his glorious Instagram know how. She's sure he knows a few things she doesn't, given his Ax Gray Insta alter-ego, but she can also manage just fine on her own.

"That's a nice offer, but no. That's not why I texted you."

Alex Bardot realizes he's been offering to teach this chick about digital strategy. While she's standing there, her nipples visible through her white tank top. She looks edible in that coverall look she's got going on. The grease on her forehead is a *look*.

What the fuck, dude? Get it together. Play it cool, get it together, tap this ass, and get out. They have an understanding. They're both adults.

"I, I like your, whatever that is," he comments on her jumpsuit.

Her hands find their way to the waistband, and she slides it off, kicking it across the floor of the workshop. She's left standing in a pair of boots, her underwear, and that greasy white tank top. He's into it, for sure.

Alex feels literal saliva pool in his mouth. He just, ugh, he needs one of her tits in his mouth. Is he drooling? He better not be drooling.

"Hey," she snaps her fingers at him. Did he just doze off?

Alex pulls himself together. Enough. He pulls the same move he did the other week, and saunters forward to lift her up around his waist. She grins.

Dimples.

His fingers tighten on her thighs, digging in, and she squirms as she locks her ankles around his lower back. Her crotch aligns with his dick, which has been getting harder throughout this encounter, and she can feel every part of him through the mesh fabric of his athletic shorts. She grinds into him a bit.

He's insatiable. He wants her over every surface of this garage. Hell, he'd have her against that car she's been working on.

Her fingers tangle themselves into his hair and she pulls him in for a thirsty fucking *kiss* that's a lot of teeth and tongue and him clawing at her back a lot. Callie pulls back to yank her tank top up off over her head, because *he* hasn't done it yet and she's all about strategy and efficiency. Her breasts bounce freely. She hasn't been wearing a bra.

Alex pulls her forward a bit and bends down to pull one of those delicious, dusky nipples between his lips, bringing a hand around to play with the one not receiving special attention from his tongue.

Callie finds this whole encounter to be much better than her Hitachi, and throws her head back as she gasps. His tongue is magic. She knew this already, after their locker room encounter, and had gotten off maybe once or twice to the memory of it. Hot, wet heat fills the space at the apex of her thighs, and she gets more delicious friction as she bucks into his hips.

"God, you taste like the best parts of Christmas," he groans, pulling off her nipple with a wet sound.

She tilts her head at him, not bothering to make a remark about her experience growing up without holidays, and sure, she knows about the concept of Santa, but she can't relate.

She leans in to bite his earlobe. "I would rather like it," she whispers, hot and breathy, "if you would fuck my throat, and then take me up against this vehicle," she leans down and sucks at his pulse point, "and fuck," a light bite to his shoulder, "my pussy. Until I can't walk tomorrow."

She leans back to make eye contact with him. Okay, okay, he can do this, he can play this game, it's one he's done many times before. Familiarity once more. He can *do* rough.

Chapter Eight

He unhooks her from his waist and drops her to the ground. His hand snakes its way to her ponytail, where he tugs, pulling downwards. She gets the message, getting to her knees on the concrete floor in front of him. Time for her to make good on that text.

Callie's decent at this part. As long as he doesn't come in her mouth. She's not a huge fan of when they do that. It rarely ever tastes good, and guys just don't get that, and they're never conscientious enough to change their diet.

Her fingers hook under the black mesh of his shorts, pulling them down to find a pair of tight grey briefs, a visible wet patch showing through the fabric. She grins up at him through her eyelashes, and he thinks he could come in his pants from this sight alone.

She mouths his dick through the fabric of his briefs, what a tease, before tugging down to free him, and he's just super grateful right now. To whatever deity there is, he's grateful.

Let's be real here. He's massive. She can't fit him all in her mouth. She'll do her best. But she's got to make use of tongue here, and use her hands to make up for the lost surface area and everything.

She licks up the underside. He's all soft and warm. She finds she likes this part, because she can sense his muscles turn to jelly. He relaxes a bit into her, but keeps his hand on the back of her head, guiding her against him, before she attempts to deep throat him and his eyes fly open.

She multitasks, covering as much ground as she can, his dick as far back possible in her throat as possible, her hand grasping the base of him as she moves, fucking him up into her mouth with precision and finesse.

He looks down, and thinks he sees a halo around this chick's head. She has to be an angel. This is otherworldly. This is a fucking religious experience. He'll go to church this Sunday, he swears.

"Oh my god, you look so fucking pretty on my cock, yes, fuck," he groans, breaking the silence with some necessary dirty talk.

Her lips surround him in a wet heat, and he can't take it. It's not that he doesn't enjoy getting blown. She's sucking his soul out of his cock like promised, but he'd like to get straight to the point.

He pulls her off his dick by her ponytail, leaving her gasping, saliva dripping onto her chin, her lips red and swollen, her pupils wide. A satisfied smile plays at the corner of her lips.

"Yes, your highness?" she murmurs, still kneeling before him. If this were anyone else, he wouldn't have stood for this sass. But it's her.

"Oh, shut the fuck up," he growls, pulling her up to her feet by her ponytail and transferring their tryst over to the single car in the garage. She leans over it, resting her elbows on the hood and widening her stance a bit.

"Let's fool around," Callie flirts as she kicks off her lacy underwear, leaving her boots on.

He waddles up behind her, his shorts still down around his thighs. "You want it raw?"

"God, yeah."

Alex runs a hand over the soft, freckled skin of her perky ass, down the cleft of her backside, and slides a finger into her cunt, to find her sopping wet. He adds a second finger, and she sloshes around him a bit as she bucks backwards into the intrusion.

"Let's *go,*" she whines. He teases her for a moment, sliding his fingers out before placing the tip of his dick to her entrance, and only pressing in. She throws a frustrated glance over her shoulder, trying to take more of him in, but he holds her still by placing a firm hand on her waist. She keens at the sensation of him stretching her entrance, knowing she's inches away from absolution.

"I swear, you're going to pay for this," she snaps at him, but mid-sentence he just, impales her. He uses the leverage on her waist to pull her back onto him so that he goes full in to the hilt in a matter of milliseconds.

She thinks he's maybe knocked the air out of her, because she takes a second to catch her breath after that. Oh wow, that's deep. She places her hands at the edge of the car, getting ready for the imminent thorough fucking she knows he's about to bestow upon her.

He takes a moment to collect himself, because the sensation is a lot for him too. And after a moment, he pulls out, thrusts back in, and begins.

Callie appreciates it when a guy knows how to fuck, but not jackhammer style. The jackhammer style is for the *weak.* This is the type of rough fucking that stops her breathing in a really, really satisfying way. With a hand on her waist and another finding its way to grip back into her ponytail, he's able to get a pretty good control on the situation, bucking into her with a satisfying slap with every thrust. He enjoys the visual of her ass jiggling a bit from this angle.

His eyes settle on a little mole on her upper back, one he didn't notice before, likely because she had a sports bra on the last time they did this. Now, he's able to truly appreciate the expanse of bare skin spread in front of him. In fact, there's freckles all across her shoulders.

With every thrust, he elicits a deep, satisfying moan from her.

The sounds rise exponentially. He hopes to fuck her coworkers are gone for the day.

Deep within her, he is hitting that spot again. Her thighs shake.

"Do you like this?" he asks her, leaning in.

She nods for some reason. Because she does like it. It's because he's losing absolute control behind her. They're both losing control together.

"God, yes."

"You're so tight, how wet were you? Were you wet for me?"

"Yes, yes," she's whispering.

She realizes she's going to come with no clitoral stimulation. This never happens.

But she likes the idea of this disgraced prince-turned-Instagram fitness model with clear daddy issues, fucking her into a fresh, new existence. She's brand new. She can forget her name, she can forget her feelings, and for a blissful, sweet blissful few moments, something else replaces that empty void the size of a black hole. Lust, maybe. Want. It's good enough for her, and she doesn't want to over think it because she's coming dangerously close to that precipice.

"Oh my god, I think I'm going to –" she whimpers a bit.

"Do it," he grabs her waist harder, her pulls her ponytail, pulls her back flush up against his chest, his dick discovering magical new places inside of her, and, yep that's it.

She's coming, her mouth wide in shock, a soft gasp.

"How's that for the royal treatment," he murmurs into her throat. "Mind if I finish?"

She nods. He slides back into her, and she winces slightly, her cunt still throbbing, red, and swollen. It doesn't take him long before he's grunting above her, painting her insides with his come.

He stays inside her until he softens, and stumbles out of her. As she falls forward a bit, losing her balance, the car lets out a distinct *beep* followed by the sound of a loud whooping alarm.

"Ugh, that weird car alarm again," she grumbles, but doesn't make a move to turn it off.

It takes a moment for his vision to focus, and he realizes he recognizes this car. And that alarm.

Uh.

It's a white Shelby GT350, with blue stripes. He *knows* this car.

She's still leaning over the hood, recuperating, but he pulls his shorts back up and shuffles around to get a decent look at the license plate with the recognizable custom lettering.

His suspicions are confirmed, and he makes a choked sound of complete shock and . . . he curses as she gazes over at him through half-lidded eyes, the beeps filling the silence of the garage.

"Callie, we just fucked on . . . Al?"

Chapter Nine

Alex looks forward to seeing her when she comes to pick up her paleo delivery.

He supposes she's an enjoyable break from his usual routine.

"Your accent," he remarks one day. It's not a question. He's curious.

"I was–*am*–an orphan. I don't actually know," she tells him, tension in her voice as she pulls her hair up into a bun and peers into the fridge. "Can we not talk about it now? One day."

"One day," he murmurs, not sure what that agreement entails. He rests his eyes on the exposed skin at the nape.

They say that it takes 21 days to form a habit, although other research says it's more like 66 days or something. Let's be real. Most of us say we're going to start a diet and 48 hours later fall face first into a box of Thin Mints.

Any way. It takes 34 days for Callie and Alex Bardot to form the habit of fucking each other, and they fall comfortably into this pattern.

When orgasms are involved, it is easy to be constant.

It's an unspoken schedule, but they do it Tuesday, Thursday, and Saturday, if she isn't going out with friends. If she goes out on Saturday, they sometimes fuck after Sunday brunch. She has half a mind to include these sexcapades in her bullet journal, next to the little red dots she uses to track her cycle.

It goes something like this, for the both of them:

Callie: 7:00am. Wake up. Stretch. Go for a run. Shower. Make oatmeal. Stretch. Teach sunrise vinyasa. Head over to Haven's. Do her own yoga practice down by the beach. See a family walking along the water, parents cradling a baby. She folds over into child's pose, tears at the corners of her eyes.

Alex: 5:00am. Wake up. Run. Head to the gym. Management meetings with Stanley and Baxter. Get roasted because his follower count isn't where it needs to be. Workouts. Teach his own classes. Run again until he feels like he might vomit. Sign a contract with another sponsor toting some new fitness enhancer, the equivalent of sawdust-filled flour bags.

And then . . .

Text Message Received *:* hey

"Fuck, tell me how wet you are right now."

"God, you're so big. Stretch me so *fucking* full."

"Fucking take it so good in your *throat* ."

"You like it when I sit on your face?"

"That's right, you take it so fucking good."

"Fucking use me, god, pull my hair *just* like that."

And it's simple.

They've got it down to a T, they light their bat signals, and they'll appear within the hour, having mastered the art of teleportation.

They've become super tactical in the way they get each other off, too. It's like a competition at this point.

"I swear to God, if you come before me, you're eating me out until I come at least twice on your tongue, you absolute fuck face."

Its peak efficiency in casual hookups. Fast food orgasms.

There's one time where she's astride him, dick hitting home base, and they're both on their phones. He's checking his Instagram direct messages with his left hand while his right thumb is busy circling her clit. She's on Wiki How, reading up on how to get her GED.

At that time, the pace is so steady and synchronous that they're able to throw their phones to the side and lean into each other, climaxing in unison.

One night, it surprised Callie to find him hovering outside Haven's garage, of his own accord, leaning against the entryway. This isn't their modus operandi. They have a *system*.

You don't fuck with the system.

But he looks tired, with dark circles, a sheen and a pallor upon his skin; he looks like one time when she was nine years old and she found a starving kitten in the desert. She took it back to her makeshift campsite and tried to nurse it back to health. It ran away the next morning.

Callie wipes her greasy hands off with a dirty towel and approaches him, tilting her head in curiosity.

"What's up?" her voice is almost gentle. Almost.

"Don't be nice to me," he tells her that night.

She's surprised she would describe their encounters as *nice*. In fact, the communication they have mid-coitus is obscene.

She supposes they've been amicable.

But that isn't what he means, is it?

So, when he goes to graze his fingertips at her temple as he lies beneath her, she swats his hand away.

When his hands find their way to her hips and he doesn't grip hard enough to leave a bruise, instead he seems to almost caress her. She grabs his wrists and pins them to the garage floor.

When he makes sounds indicating pleasure, she muffles them with her palm, turning to press his face into the concrete beneath.

After all, she's just following instructions.

Chapter Ten

They run into each other down by the pier one day. It's overcast and windy and there are whitecaps on the waves. He's coming off a photo shoot for his dumb Instagram page. She greets him with an eye roll, because his dark board shorts are slung way too low on his hips for any self-respecting human.

She buys a soft serve ice cream, and they fall into step beside each other, going for a quick stroll down the boardwalk.

He makes a disparaging comment about dairy, wondering what happened to her paleo diet.

She shoves the soft serve into his face at that, smearing it across his chin. The white mess covers his five o'clock shadow.

It should have been cute. But they end up bickering, because he's frustrated and cranky after the photo shoot and still covered in tanning oil.

They end up in one of the changing room huts, fucking on a dirty bench. She licks the ice cream off his jaw line while his fingers weave their way into her ponytail.

Callie ends up with a UTI, and doesn't text him for a week after that.

What's also efficient is the locale for these trysts. It's always either the garage, the yoga studio, or the gym. Conveniently after hours.

They've successfully fucked for three months without ever seeing the inside of the other's home.

The problem is, the more often they do this outside the privacy of a bedroom, the more likely they are to get caught.

"What are you doing?" comes the flat, disgruntled voice of Rita McKinnon, a fellow mechanic at Haven's.

Callie is up on her workbench, legs wrapped around Alex's waist while he leans her over wrenches and ratchet extenders and a needle scaler.

They're not fucking yet, but to an outside observer, it's pretty clear where this encounter was headed.

"Oh, fuck. Sorry, Rita."

Rita tells them to clean up after themselves and gives the duo an eye roll. She slams the door shut as she departs.

They didn't finish, just got dressed and left.

Dean corners Callie in their shared stucco cottage.

"I looked up 'douchelord' on Urban Dictionary, Callie, and pretty sure I found that guy's photo cross-posted with the entry for 'fuckboy.' What are you doing?"

"I'm a grown woman and can make my own decisions," she replies, shrugging.

At the yoga studio, Penn accosts her as well. Rita had told Dean, who had told Penn, and chaos ensued. Fuck group texts.

"Stop projecting the issues you've got with your twisted little love triangle onto me," Callie snaps at Penn, referring to recent drama involving a one-night stand between Dean and Rita.

She's not used to people caring about what she does.

She's not used to people caring about her.

"He's totally got issues, Callie. You can pick your friends more carefully." Dean tries to tell her later when they're curled up on the couch together, watching Netflix and eating takeout.

"I'm not *friends* with the guy," she shrugs. "We're just fucking."

"He's estranged from his family."

"He owns a gym across the street from his family's business. What do we make of that?" Callie side-eyes him.

"Affordable real estate?" Dean offers.

"So you're both seeing other people, right?"

Callie can't speak for Alex, but when she tells Dean, "yeah, of course I am," it's a lie.

———

The next time they fuck, they're in his locker room, and he's balls deep with her up around his waist. He's giving her a hickey near her collarbone.

"Are you seeing other people?" Callie asks him. He stops mid-thrust and lifts his lips from her skin, panting hard.

"What the fuck?" he responds, his voice rough. His fingers press a little harder into her thighs.

"I said, are you seeing other people?" Their eyes meet.

He pulls out of her, flips her around to press her flush up against the row of metal lockers, and continues fucking her from behind. Her fingers scramble to get a grip on the slippery surface, her cheek cold against the metal.

They don't speak for the rest of the encounter.

Hours later, after she's gone home to shower, and she's wiped his come off her thighs and she's lying in bed taking a GED practice test, she receives a text from him.

Cross Fit, Rock Hard Abs: no I'm not

The more time they spend together, she notices cracks on his surface. Sometimes those fissures run deep.

Sweat on his brow, when he doesn't appear to have been working out. A tremor in his hands. A twitch under his left eye.

It's like how dust gathers at the top of a bookshelf you pass each day. And then one day you find yourself unsettled by how much dust has gathered. But the dust has always been there, so why do you care about the dust now?

There's an evening where Callie snaps at him, her suspicions boiling over to the surface. She grabs his arm and rolls up the sleeves of his hoodie to check for needle marks.

Alex's eyes widen in surprise as she prods the skin at the crease at his elbow, finding nothing.

Chapter Eleven

They're at the Asana Peace and Serenity studio this time, and they've just finished fucking on one of the yoga mats in the practice room. She had gotten creative with her use of the downward dog pose.

She pulls on her sweatpants after he's charitably licked her clean.

"What's the deal with your manager? Stanley? Do you even like the stuff he has you do?"

"Like what?"

"You know, the weird photo shoots. The contracts with the shady companies. Your ridiculous workouts. The Ax Gray bullshit. Is that who you want to be?"

"It's just business, Callie. It's business. We both benefit." He's not meeting her gaze as he pulls his shirt on over his chiseled torso.

"How do you benefit?" She laces her sneakers aggressively, her voice sharp.

"I–I get to own my own gym. I'm really independent."

She can hear the tension in his tone.

He can feel the pressure in his own chest.

"Are you?" He meets her eyes at that, and something

unspoken passes between them. The tension dissipates. They depart the studio, side by side.

———

Callie realizes they've both reached critical mass without knowing how they've arrived there.

Callie realizes when she hits "send current location" and it's neither the yoga studio nor Haven's. It's her cottage.

You don't fuck with the system.

It dawns on her when he's buried inside of her, and she realizes their pace is slow and languid. He's not thrusting into her, or talking dirty. In fact, there's only two words they exchange here.

"Callie."

"Alex."

His lips are lazy against her throat. Lazy against her forehead. Her fingers caress the vertebrae of his spine softly.

Her gasps and the murmurs he makes as he kisses her temple are the only sounds in the room. She supposes she can hear a bird chirping outside. The morning sun casts a soft light onto the white sheets where they're tangled together.

She realizes she hasn't shaved her legs in a few days, and neither of them gives a fuck.

The realization dawns on her they're *in a bed*. But more glaringly, when did this become a *slow* thing?

Chapter Twelve

Alex Bardot does Cross Fit.

It's who he is. He's great at what he does.

He can do a lot of push-ups in one go. You should see this dude go. He's a fucking beefcake. A brick house.

He can't keep up with the influx of messages from public relations representatives trying to take advantage of his *influencer status*. Bendy female Instagram fitspo models are crawling all over his DMs.

He has his pick. He could have anyone.

Alex Bardot does Cross Fit.

He began, years ago, working out to soothe the lingering poison in his veins, the bile in his throat. You know, like, endorphins make you happy. Happy people don't . . . kill their families. Some Elle Woods wisdom for you there.

He could hear the muffled voices of his parents through the walls of their old estate. Arguing about his deceased, irresponsible grandfather. Anakin Dalton, a notorious film noir movie star, had some issues. Arguing over Alex's father's unsafe racing practices and his, you know, other less-than-legal practices.

As mentioned, Alex Bardot has some tormented familial shit going on.

But he also could hear the more hushed tones of his parents when the topic switched to *him*.

He's troubled. What's wrong? What's wrong with Alex Bardot? We need to talk about Alex Bardot. He won't talk to the other kids in school. He's always reading books, he's quiet. Why does he stare at the stars, as if they might speak back? Why's he so quiet?

And he wants to crawl out of his own skin, in the memory of this, as it clouds his vision and he forgets where he is and why he's here on planet Earth and it's twenty years ago.

He's fine, he wants to yell. He's fine, I'm fine! I really am. Why are you so worried?

After all, they want what is best for him. They're concerned and mean well. He supposes . . . he knows they do.

They mean well.

That doesn't mean adults don't fuck up here and there, you know.

But parents *usually* mean well. At least in this case.

Even when Sandra, his mother, is throwing a hair dryer at his father. When Max Bardot, his father, hightails it out of there, his engine revving, and it's 3:00 a.m.

He catches his mother one night, out on the balcony, watching his father leave. Her husband. Again and again. This happens a lot until one night, his father doesn't return.

So when it gets like this, Alex Bardot is doing his burpees. As many as push-ups and squats, he can. Then he crawls the rope until his palms are raw. His muscles shake as he rows.

His heartbeat racing, and the endorphins flood his veins. They flood his veins and he can feel nothing else but the surge of adrenaline, the surge, the surge.

And there's the voice, the voice that grounds him, that has lured him into greatness, of course.

The voice of asset manager Stanley, at the edge of the gym, urging him on. And Alex relaxes into that voice. It's proud. It sees his potential. That voice sees all the great things he knows he can become. Listen, Instagram fitness models make bank on those sponsorships.)

So Ax Gray does Cross Fit.

Moments alone, he cherishes *those*. His apartment is a few blocks away from the gym. It's nice, a lot of stainless steel and nice dark granite countertops. There's fucking *shiplap* on the walls. He got inspired by an episode of Fixer-Upper. There's not a lot of *stuff* in this apartment, but there are parts of him here. Small parts of him.

He'll allow his fingers to trace over the spines of well-loved books. Books he hasn't opened in years, but they line the shelves near his bed.

He'll sit, cross legged, in front of these books. They're familiar to him.

Embarrassment spreads as gooseflesh across his arms, alone in his apartment, as he catches himself appreciating the memories of the words of the likes of Carl Sagan and Michio Kaku and Brian Greene. It's silly. It's so silly. Why is he drawn to this stuff, anyway? Why does he look to the stars? Stars. The stars are stupid. The stars don't have the answers.

You know what, fuck stars. He goes out to the living room, where he has a wall mount installed, and does a bunch of pull-ups until his biceps quiver.

And so that's another night gone, when he doesn't allow himself to open one of those adored books, with the creases at their spines and the pages yellow with age.

But they sit near his bed, so that when Alex Bardot goes to sleep, he allows his eyes to drift over those well-loved books, as heavy-lidded eyes shut and he falls into a restless sleep. He wakes each morning in a cold sweat; the sheets tangled in knots around his legs.

Ax Gray does Cross Fit.

They're in her cottage again, one Sunday morning.

"I have this dream," she tells him, running her toes up along his calf muscles.

He gazes at her as he leans up on an elbow, nodding for her to continue.

"I've told no one. It sounds too weird, maybe."

"I won't think it's weird."

"I'm underwater. And I'm alone. I'm floating in the water, and at first, I'm afraid, afraid I'm going to drown. But then I breathe. It's not even like I have gills or anything." she stops to laugh, expecting Alex to laugh as well, but finds him silent and transfixed. She exhales and looks away, continuing, "I can just breathe there. It's the calmest thing ever. Maybe in another life, I was a fish."

"Maybe."

"Do you dream?"

"Constantly." his fingers play with the short tendrils of hair at the nape. It tickles, but nicely.

She wants to ask him to extrapolate. She wants him to tell her everything, but his gaze traps her and tells her everything she needs to know just in that precise moment, and she doesn't press him.

His eyes are sad and tired.

She knows that look all too well as she has seen those eyes before.

Chapter Thirteen

The next day, Ax Gray uploads a typography graphic to his Instagram account.
CATCH FITNESS
NOT FEELINGS.
The type is grungy, white on a black background.
He deletes it 27 minutes after he uploads it.
The damage is done, but not how he might expect.
"I keep a close eye on my assets, as you know," Stanley is pacing the shared office of High Octane Cross Fit, running his wrinkly fingers along the edge of Alex's desk.
Baxter is sneering in the corner, smug and proud that Alex fucked up.
"Tell me about this girl, this yoga instructor, you know so . . . intimately."
"What girl?"
"The girl that ridiculous Instagram post was directed towards, before you deleted it like a guilty little boy with his hands caught in the cookie jar," Stanley hisses. Alex imagines a forked tongue slipping out of those thin lips. Baxter chortles in the office's corner.
"I don't know what you're talking about," Alex stammers.

"You ruined a good editorial calendar," Stanley laments. "And you lost eleven followers with that little charade. Nobody likes typography these days."

Alex scowls a bit, but stays silent. He bets Baxter spilled the beans on his trysts with Callie. He racks his brain to remember a time when they could have fucked up, might have stepped out of line and gotten caught unaware . . . but Baxter is a silent predator. He's pulled shit like this before to undermine him. It's hopeless.

"Stick to the *system*, son," Stanley leans over Alex's desk, breathing into his personal space in a very fucked up way. "Don't mess with it. Or else."

So here's the thing. Callie is used to being alone. She did it for years. But she's gotten used to this familiar, little habitual–whatever this thing was she had going on with Alex Bardot. It had become as easy as brushing her teeth in the morning. He was like her morning face wash. Her Hitachi had gathered dust under her bed somewhere.

So when he hasn't texted her in a solid week, she feels it. She feels that break in habit. Maybe inviting him over to her cottage had crossed a line. It sucks, because she had canceled her paleo subscription and can't use the pick-up fridge as an excuse to go check out the gym. She doesn't want to seem needy or anything. She can't appear too clingy.

That's a man's job.

She goes to two sessions of Bikram on one day, to sweat out all her unreleased frustration. Next, she goes back to the fucking Jamba Juice, which she hasn't been to in a hot minute. As she's hovering by the pick-up counter, she turns back to see him at the entrance of the store. Their eyes meet through the dirty glass of the front door, and he pauses, his hand on the door frame, before he turns on his heel and walks away.

She makes a noise between a scoff and a gasp. Callie abandons her smoothie at the counter to chase him across the street.

She grabs at his gym bag where it's hanging over his back, pulling him back towards her. They stop in the middle of the crosswalk.

"What the fuck, dude?" she snaps at him as she walks around to stand in front of him, blocking his path. He doesn't meet her eyes. His face is expressionless as he looks everywhere but at her, fidgeting with the strap of his gym bag.

She hits him on the arm in frustration. "Talk to me."

He doesn't.

"Alex!" she smacks his arm again.

"Go away," he tells her. Where the fuck is this coming from? Why is she so surprised? This is *exactly* what she should have expected from day one. But still, what the hell?

"What the hell?" her voice drops a bit, it's softer now.

Before she processes what she's doing, she's standing on her toes to press their lips together.

Cars are beeping because the light has now turned green and they're blocking the road. She lifts a middle finger to the traffic.

He doesn't kiss her back.

She pulls away again, brow furrowed and tears pooling in her eyes. "Alex?"

He won't look at her, instead placing his hands on her shoulders and lifting her up and out of his way, continuing across the street.

She's left alone in the middle of the crosswalk, with bile in her throat.

But it's like she told Dean. She was never friends with Ax Gray.

Chapter Fourteen

It's nights like these.

And she curls over into her side, in her empty bed, and though it's eighty degrees outside, the emptiness and the cold consume her.

It's nights like these, where the fear that she may tumble backward into her previous existence looms over her like a dark shadow.

Would she be homeless again? What if her friends up and left? What if Dean decided he hated her and wanted a new roommate? What if Haven fired her?

She walks a tightrope of existence some days. Days where she teeters on the brink of sanity, looking down into the cavernous depths beneath her. Placing one foot in front of the other, arms outstretched in a desperate plea for balance. Balance.

Loneliness could be just a stumble away. She may trip and fall headfirst into it. She feels as if nobody may ever understand.

This truth must be hers and hers alone. This song of emptiness is one she must sing only to herself. A song nobody else could ever fathom. Isn't it?

And so she curls up on her side, in her bed that feels altogether too hot and also too cold, and she cries into the sheets.

Though no tears fall.

She winces, her eyes shut.

And she realizes that the way she used to calm herself back out in the desert is here, so close to her doorstep.

And though it may be far past midnight, Callie bikes down to the beach. The moon casts a glow on the dark waters and the waves hit the shore with a calming trickle. She kicks off her sandals and steps into the surf's edge.

Her toes dig into the sand, and the water goes up around her ankles, ebbing and flowing with her.

Callie no longer needs to imagine an ocean to survive. She has one right here.

She just breathes.

The feeling in her chest. It's raw, it's clawing at her edges, and it's still there. It hasn't gone away.

But she learned long ago, it isn't *about* making that feeling go away.

In her mind's eye, she sees herself as a child. A five-year-old girl, eyes puffy and red after escaping yet another foster home.

And that five-year-old girl is lonely and sad, and yet so determined and persistent and full of hope. That girl is crying, huddled in an abandoned building at the edge of a town in the desert.

In her mind's eye, Callie embraces this little girl.

"I've got you," Callie whispers.

The water is cool at her feet.

"Stick it out, kid," she tells herself. The little girl in her mind's eye struggles, whimpering helplessly as children do.

And finally, as a rough wave hits her up around her calves, the tears begin to flow. Steady streaming down her face. She bows her chin to her chest, her hair falling into her face.

"I've got you, sweetheart," she murmurs, her arms wrapping their way around her chest, clasping herself into an embrace of her own making. "I'm not letting go."

Bile.

A claw that grips his stomach.

A quivering claw grips his stomach, the other crawls around to the back of his eyeballs.

And then another claw at his throat. He'll scratch at the delicate skin there. It's so *itchy*.

Another claw, snaking up to scrape the back of his neck. Why the fuck is this happening?

The real reason he can't stand being in public? The tears that prickle at the corner of his eyes, precisely when shit like this happens.

Many times, Alex Bardot ends up bent over a trash can, trying to wretch whatever this horrible sensation is up and out of his throat, but nothing comes out. He just ends up spitting onto an empty black trash bag in frustration, tears welling once more in his eyes.

He'll stumble into the gym bathroom, stand in front of the sink, and try to splash cold water on his face.

The surge, the surge.

He makes eye contact with himself in the mirror, but he doesn't recognize the eyes that stare back.

The surge, the surge.

He slaps himself back into place. His own clammy palm contacts his cheek.

He trips as he makes his way back out into the cavernous gym. The walls are high above him, reminiscent of a cathedral nave. The concrete bricks are painted back but faded with age. The floor is covered with speckles of grey.

Like stars across the night sky.

Chapter Fifteen

Callie settles back into her daily routine. If you're under him, you're not getting over him, you know? Not that—let's be clear—not that there was anything to *get over*.

She travels up the coast with Penn for a weekend to take a yoga instructor training session specifically on pre-natal yoga. Plus, the more teacher training hours she has under her belt, the better.

She continues to practice for the GED. She's mastered the art of meal planning, which was one of her resolutions for this new year, and she's been failing miserably. No, food subscription services do not count. She's been kidding herself. She spends Sunday afternoons in her cottage kitchen, sweating up a storm while she tries to roast vegetables and boil eggs.

She also takes a holiday with Dean out to Catalina Island. They get an Airbnb and sit out on the whitewashed balcony, the spring air fresh with the smell of the surf and far-off french fries from the tourist boardwalk.

"What happened to that dude? The Instagram fitness model?" Dean asks her.

Callie shrugs, drinking her lemonade through a blue, bendy straw. "Men suck."

Dean laughs at that. "Well, did you have any fun with him, at least?"

She grins over at him, nudging her sunglasses down the bridge of her nose so she's looking at him from over the lens frames. "He was a terrific lay. Don't worry about that."

"I'm here if you need to chat, Callie," he tells her. She throws her head back with a chuckle.

"If we're going to chat about anything, it should be about my tormented childhood, but not right now, maybe," she jokes.

She wants to *joke* about the past sometimes. Like, she can't change it, you know?

And sometimes the best way to heal from a haunted past is to laugh about it. Not weirdly. Just in a this-happened-to-me-I-can't-change-it-and-I'm-functioning-now sort of way.

Later, as they're making more lemonade in the kitchen. They may or may not spike it with some vodka, but that's neither here nor there. Dean grabs her and pulls her in for a tight hug.

She takes a minute to settle into it. Her initial instinct is to squirm away from him.

But then, she smiles into his shoulder, into the vulnerability relaxing, and embraces him back.

As the night goes on, Dean spills the beans on the *Big Brother*-level drama surrounding his tumultuous love triangle with Penn and Rita. Everyone's having a fucking quarter life crisis these days. He's waxing poetic about broken hearts and caring about people and where he fits in and *what does this all mean?*

"I don't know. Everyone should be happy. I don't want to upset them. Someone will end up with a broken heart. It's breaking *my* heart. You know about that," Dean says, meeting her gaze as he drunkenly leans back into his patio chair.

"You can't please everyone. Also, Cross Fit guy didn't break my heart," she clarifies to Dean. He nods in understanding. "It's," her voice falters, and she looks off into the distance, out to the moon over the Avalon Bay harbor, "I let someone in. It's tough when you bring someone into your life and then you lose them. I guess." She sips her spiked lemonade.

"People aren't cars, Callie," he blurts. She blinks, meeting his warm brown eyes. "And," he presses his mouth into a thin line before continuing, "you don't have to be ' *in love'* with them to want to, you know, fix them."

She wants to fight him at that, because he's—how dare—but. The American southwest is where she grew up. Callie is an auto mechanic. She mends broken parts and creates new things from old all the time. When she was a kid, she was a sucker for abandoned animals. Like that one kitten, she had tried to nurse back to health before it ran away. But *people* aren't broken car parts or starving kittens. That's something she's come to learn over the past few years, as she gets to, you know, *know* more people.

Sometimes, the toughest thing to hear is the truth. A very hard fucking pill to swallow. You know, that's why when girlfriends tell us over brunch that the dude we're dating is a misogynistic fuckboy, we just really do not want to hear it and leave the group chat for a solid week.

A hard fucking pill to swallow.

Callie and Dean throw a house party as spring ends and summer looms.

Dean's out on the patio with the grill, taking orders. There are a *lot* of gluten-free buns and veggie bean burgers. Callie's tipsy already, thanks to the sangria, and she grabs a bottle of Jose Cuervo and sauntering back into their living room, announcing to the party, "Tequila shots!"

That's how Callie ends up lying across her own kitchen counter, Kinsey Conrad (the yoga studio's social media coordinator) licking a long, thick stripe of tequila off the bare skin of Callie's lower abdomen. They had agreed to a little contest: auto shop social media management vs. yoga social media management.) Who will emerge victorious from the very classy art of body shots? Callie squirms with delight, pulling Kinsey down to her mouth for a quick soft kiss before they pull apart laughing. Kinsey disengages, pinching Callie's cheek.

Later, Callie goes back into the living room, swinging her hips to the beat of the Spotify playlist, before she climbs into Penn's lap, because fuck it. She's only young once. Callie places her hands on either side of his stubbly face and pulls him in for a sloppy kiss. Which, thankfully, for the greater good, he does not reciprocate.

Instead, he pulls her down and away from those delicious lips.

"This isn't what you want, Callie," Penn tells her, and she smiles at him.

Instead, he curls her up onto his lap, so that it tucked her head under his chin. He embraces her here, his arms wrapped around her. Through half-lidded eyes, she sees him motion to someone in the background, and a few minutes later, Dean is coming to sit down next to them, placing a cool washcloth over her forehead and handing her a glass of ginger ale.

"You guys think I'm dumb," she hiccups. Is the room spinning?

Dean laughs at this. "This doesn't come close to any of the dumb shit I've done."

Penn looks down at her, squeezing his arms around her. "It's okay not to be okay," he whispers into her scalp. Some mindfulness bullshit here, but she hates that even in this tequila-haze, she knows he's right.

Maybe don't be friends with yoga instructors unless you want everything to sound like a Deepak Chopra tape.

"We're your friends, Callie," Dean reaches over to jab her shoulder.

As he says this, Callie feels it again. She wants to squirm away, that feeling in the pit of her stomach, the feeling that she wants to rip herself away from these people, the people that say they care about her.

She's done it before. She can do it again.

But this time, this time, she closes her eyes and tells the feeling to chill the fuck out for a second. It coils in her veins, and she recognizes it as fear, but she swallows it. Because even though she's afraid, maybe it's okay to trust that there's maybe at least one person in the world–two, here, in this case–who might give a shit about her?

She *can* be alone. She *knows* she can do just fine on her own.

But the thing is, in this moment right here, she doesn't have to.

Ah yes, the magic of tequila. Doesn't always come with a side effect of intuitive epiphanies, but when it does...

Chapter Sixteen

Alex lies back in his bed, his head up against the headboard, scrolling through his Instagram feed.

He finds his way to his iCloud photo stream, and as he scrolls through it, he sees it.

The image Callie had sent months prior, when she was luring him to the garage for that first booty call of theirs.

He'd saved this image for god knows what reason.

It was a selfie, taken with both arms outstretched. She had tilted the camera up above her for that optimal angle, and tilted her head, her smile wide, her eyes crinkled shut. A strap of her white tank top was falling off her shoulder in this photo. There was a bit of a grease smear on her forehead.

What the fuck had he done? How dare he let Baxter and Stanley get under his skin like that?

A super logical voice in the back of his head tells him to just, you know, say sorry to her, maybe.

For what?

He goes out to his living room, back to his wall mount, and finds that even pull-ups don't soothe whatever the fuck this feeling is coursing through his veins.

It's a new feeling. He decides he doesn't like it.

Okay, consider that thing that happens in the movies where two people run into each other on the sidewalk, and then they try to side-step each other but they keep blocking each other and it's a whole awkward *thing* until one of them acquiesces? Which usually takes, like, three years to happen?

So, with that visual in mind, let's remember the fact that Callie's place of employment is directly across the street from Alex Bardot's. She's bound to walk by it.

Occasionally.

"No, after you," Callie motions.

"I couldn't–" Alex begins.

"Oh, you couldn't? Couldn't possibly pass me by?" Callie snarls.

"Please, you go," Alex motions for her to walk by him.

Callie may be small, but she's a fighter. Don't let her yoga physique fool you. She knows how to use her fists. If she wants, she can lift.

See, mindfulness and breathing through anger and all that shit is super easy when you're sitting on a comfy yoga mat with a scented candle going. But now, she's face to face with this dude, and everything she's been shelving deep within the confines of her mind creeps out of every crevice, and she's cornering him back up against the glass of one of his gym windows, her forearm pressed against his chest.

"I would like to say, with a lot of feeling," she announces to him, "fuck you." She punctuates this with an extra push of her forearm against his pecs.

He blinks down at her. He's surprised at the strength by which she has him pinned to the glass.

"I don't–"

"Has anyone ever told you you're an asshole? I want you to know you're an asshole."

He blinks again. "Do we have to talk about this here?"

"Oh, no, please, be my guest," she motions towards the door of his gym. She spins him to face it, and shoves him towards it, grabbing him by the back of his shirt and forcing him towards the entrance.

They stumble inside. He turns to lock the door, though for what reason, neither of them can fathom right now.

What could they get up to right now that requires a locked door?

He turns to face her, his ears the color of a beet.

"How about you give up the lease on this gym and go somewhere else, so I don't have to run into you," she says, matter-of-fact, crossing her arms across her chest.

He feels heat seep into his fingertips, into his toes, at this.

The color from Alex's ears seeps into a flush across his cheeks. "You don't know the first thing about me."

"I know enough." She kicks an errant exercise ball across the gym. It bounces. Bop. Bop. Bop.

He watches the ball bounce away, and his kettle boils over. "Not everyone can," he pants, "solve their problems," another raggedy breath, "with some deep breathing and insane flexibility!" He's spitting.

She holds up her pointer finger to jab the air. "First, you wouldn't know a tadasana from a savasana if it bit you in the ass," she's panting now as well, and holds up a second finger, "second, *second*–I don't solve my problems that way, you moron."

Alex doesn't respond. He blinks at her. How do people solve their problems again?

Callie groans. "God, you're so *fucking* dense, you know that? *Fuck* you, and while you're at it, let me give you the name of a good therapist!" She yells at him, her fists clenched. He notices there's a little vein in her forehead that's popping. Fascinating.

For a gym as big as this one, it feels pretty suffocating. The black cement walls close in on them. They stay like that for a moment, breathing evenly, now at an impasse.

And what do we do when we're at an impasse?

Alex imagines it's like a fucking neutron collision, the way they're clawing at each other, the way two unstoppable forces meet each other in the middle. They're the goddamn Large Hadron Collider.

Just speed up two particles towards each other at crazy speeds, see what happens. What could go wrong?

Chapter Seventeen

As he pulls her up around his waist, clinging to her like a goddamn life raft, she realizes their kisses taste salty. She grasps at his shoulders as she pulls away to find they're both crying, but not the sort of sobbing crying, they've got the angry tears going on that well up at the bottom of your eyes and spill over.

They spill over like the soda you filled at the beverage station and you're trying to carry it back to your table but then the liquid spills out over the edges and you've got a guilty look on your face because fuck, somebody is going to clean that up.

You don't want to be the one to clean that up; you know? What a mess.

Neither of them verbally acknowledges this, instead returning to their oral assault on each other's lips. It's a volley, where she bites his tongue. Moments later, he'll bite her lip in return.

She wraps her arms around the back of his neck, her legs interlocking at his lower back.

None of this is slow.

This is no longer a slow thing. It could have stayed a slow thing.

Could it still end up a slow thing?

So he has her up around his waist, and he walks them backward, across the expanse of the gym. They press open-mouthed kisses against each other's face in a strange jostle of tongues. He's got her so solidly up around him. (You can go years wanting to find a guy that can do the thing where he holds you up around his waist, and ugh, when you find one...)

Instead of the locker room, she finds he brings them into what appears to be an office space. Two desks on opposite sides of the room. One is clean and organized, all stainless steel and sharp lines. The other is messier, books piled atop each other. It's not the most welcoming room. (Not, uh, that the locker room was any better. But how does he get work done in here?)

There are questions brewing in the back of her throat. She's asking herself why she doesn't pull away and yell at him, why isn't she slapping him? Why is she kissing him? Why is she in this office? Why is his hard-on so distracting? Isn't she stronger than this?

She can still taste his tears. It might be because he is so warm. Maybe it's because he still feels as familiar as her morning face wash, as familiar as the sheets she rolls into to sleep at night, as familiar as a well-worn blanket you huddle under when reading a good book.

She doesn't want to let go of him. She just doesn't want to, even with every rational neuron in her brain firing at her, telling her what's right, what's the right choice?

Let's be clear: She'll be okay. Just fine.

Alex is not having a similar train of thought. Again, he's clinging to her like she's the door Rita floats on at the end of the movie and he's Jack, except Jack ends up frozen to death and at the bottom of the sea. Where's he going with this?

He brackets her in, up against the wall of the office, as she balances on his waist. His lips leave hers and he pants. His chest heaves beneath the thin cotton of his shirt.

She tilts his chin up with one finger.

"You're scared," she whispers before she even knows what she's insinuating.

"Don't," comes his voice, hoarse, before he sucks a red spot right above her collarbone. Did he remember what it does to her? Did he have that info filed away in his memory, to use as ammo in a situation like this, just to quiet her?

The damn neck thing. She can't resist, and she goes limp in his arms.

Before she can fall to the ground, he catches her, hoisting her further up the cement wall.

"Is this your office?" she asks, slanting her neck to accept his lips as they travel up the expanse of skin there.

"Yes," he murmurs above her carotid artery.

"We've never been in here," she muses. Why is she talking? Stop talking.

Less talking, more fucking. That's the system.

He hums in acknowledgment before carrying her over to the cleaner desk of the two. Her ass hits the cold stainless steel beneath her.

She's wearing a sundress today, one she had changed into after teaching a few classes at the studio. It had also been laundry day, so her underwear isn't the nicest . Not that he gives a shit.

He slides the eyelet lace of the sundress up around her waist.

"Fuck, I missed this."

"Whose fault is that?" she prods.

His brow furrows. He looks ravenous. "Lean back."

"Whatever you say, Bardot," a grin spreading on her face despite her best efforts to refrain. Alex gets to his knees in front of the desk. He pulls the cotton of her underwear down her thighs, before tossing them over his shoulder and burying his tongue deep. There, right there. She lets out an audible sigh.

"Keep that up," she tells him, threading her fingers into the hair at the back of his head and pulling him into her.

He pulls away, pressing little bites to the delicate juncture between her thighs.

"You taste," another bite to her skin, "so fucking good."

She doesn't want to admit she's been soaking wet and throbbing since she cornered him up against the window–how long has it been since then? Ten minutes?

"Does this factor into your macro or micronutrients count for the day?" She gasps as his tongue begins to circle her clit. Her hips buck up into the assault. More.

To maybe shut her up, it's not that he doesn't enjoy hearing her voice, he does, let's be clear, but when that flush spreads across her chest and up her neck and she goes limp and gasping, he likes that even better–he slides a finger in, hooking it up deep within her. He's rewarded with a fresh gush of arousal around his finger, so he adds a second one, beckoning far within her pussy.

She stops talking, alright. She spreads her legs wider across the desk. Her thighs and glutes tremble. She's so sure this is the hill she's going to die on, here, on this stainless steel desk, letting the Fuckboy of the Year eat her out with all the concentrated effort and vigor of a front loading washing machine.

It's not that she missed this. It's just that she knows how to appreciate a good lay when she's got one trapped between her muscular thighs.

She realizes she's about to come in a very new, very different way. He's hitting something indescribable. They know each other's bodies with embarrassing familiarity, even after their hiatus , but he's here toeing the limits of what he knows, for their first reunion.

Her head lolls backward, hitting the cement wall behind the desk.

"Holy-oh-my-oh, what, oh-yes," are her intelligible, coherent sounds and half words spewing out of her mouth, which feel simultaneously very dry and thick at the same time. Maybe it's because she's gasping for breath? She feels lightheaded and realizes she should maybe get a hold of her breathing, but he's got her pinned down like a beetle in an entomologist's collection tray.

"Alex," she murmurs as she hits a wave and begins to ride it.

He's stroking so fucking deep within her. She forgot how much she appreciates his long fingers.

The thing is, they had gotten used to skipping foreplay when they had been hooking up regularly. This is altogether too familiar and yet uncharted territory. Almost like when they had first fucked so many months ago.

Noises of desperation come from somewhere deep within her chest. He has half a mind to pin her to the table with his hands, but enjoys this particular reaction.

Instead, he uses his free hand to come up to meet hers, their fingers intertwining, settling on the steel surface beneath them.

"Come all over this desk," he pants, pulling away slightly, "do it, do it babe."

She thinks she might smack him for the babe comment, but who the fuck is she kidding? With the way he's puppeting her? Let him have his terms of endearment or whatever. Let him think this is whatever he thinks it is. Her fingernails embed crescent shapes in his hand. His tongue returns to her clit, beginning a strong and assured crescendo from steady licks to efficient circles and –

Yes.

Her orgasm isn't a loud one, not this one. Her eyes fly open in surprise as he pulls back, his fingers coaxing her quaking pussy through it, but pulling back to let the liquid climax erupting from her cover the desk beneath them.

Alex raises his eyebrows. She's squirted before, sure. She's no spring chicken in this department. And she's definitely squirted with him around.

But Alex thinks this is . . . the Oregon Trail, and it's a river crossing and he might want to consider caulking his wagon.

Her head drops forward onto her chest. "Oh my god," she breathes, her chest heaving. "That was a lot."

Alex nods, wide-eyed. "Fuck yeah."

"You can fuck me now, or whatever," Callie chides him, tearing her hand away from where it's been holding his and playing with her cuticles, "but after that? I'm not moving. Put your sick gains to work."

His jaw goes slack. Why else does he work out, if not to maintain ludicrous stamina during a hookup?

He gets up off his knees, standing before her and aligning their hips just so. He wraps an arm around her lower back, his muscles accommodating her small frame easily, as he slides his dick into her with a soft, wet sound.

She's so wet, there's zero resistance. But she's also tight, holding his dick in a vice grip.

"You're so..." he speaks.

"Tight?" she murmurs into his ear softly. She's gone boneless in his arms, and as he thrusts, she flops around a bit. He chokes slightly, hearing her talk like that.

She notices his reaction.

"Did you miss it?" She's fucking goading him. "How many nights did you spend with your fist wrapped around your cock? Wishing it was my wet pussy? Huh? And to think..."

He interrupts her slightly with an energetic movement. She notices it covers his forehead in a sheen of sweat, his hair plastered to his forehead.

"To think if you hadn't been such an asshole." her tone turns sharp, and she lifts her hands to scratch her fingers down his biceps, red, streaking marks in their wake.

"You don't know–," he grunts out.

"Keep fucking me like this, though, maybe stay in my good graces," her voice goes up an octave slightly.

When she orgasms a second time, it isn't as forceful. It's light and airy. She can almost feel the endorphins tickling her skin.

He pulls his cock out right before he's about to come and aims at the steel of the desk beneath them. She narrows her eyes in confusion as he covers the remnants of her earlier orgasm with his come.

To each their own?

She shifts up and over the mess, straightening her skirt down as her feet hit the floor.

"Should we clean that up?"

"No," is his terse answer.

"Isn't it your desk?"

He chortles as they depart the office space, shaking his head. "Nope."

Chapter Eighteen

"You have a choice to make, my boy," Stanley explores Alex's office area, knocking shit over in some sort of attempted machismo power play. The man knocked over the water bottle. He knocks over a container of expensive protein powder. A mini stress ball is being knocked off Alex's desk. It rolls across the linoleum, across the room, and Baxter stops it under the sole of his shoe.

"The contract you signed discusses terms relating to interpersonal relationships involving competing individuals within the fitness industry. This didn't seem to be a problem." Stanley slithers up into Alex's personal space, caging Alex in on his office chair. Alex can see every nook and cranny in the man's gross, wrinkled face. His breath is hot and swamp-like. "Until now."

"I wouldn't call her competition, she just works across the street," Alex bargains here. His neck is getting so fucking itchy.

"Quiet." Stanley snaps and ponders this for a second. "I won't have you distracted. And after this little stunt you pulled with poor Baxter and his desk," Stanley clicks his tongue.

"Poor Baxter?" Alex sputters. Baxter looks over at him from across the room, smug and satisfied with the way events are unfolding here. The redhead smoothes some of his hair back over his scalp. The amount of hair product the fucker uses is embarrassing, and this is coming from Alex, who is no stranger to the intricacies of hair care.

"Ax, just get your shit together," Stanley bites. He emphasizes this by punching the armrests of the office chair where Alex sits.

Alex flinches. "I've sold my soul to you," his voice drops, cracking. "What else do you want from me?"

"The sponsors love you. Keep them happy, keep me happy, stay focused. Stop making doe eyes at this common yoga tramp. We could pay for you to have a partnership with a prominent female individual. Is that what you want? What about that lovely entrepreneur, Sera Arlett? She has three million followers. I'm sure she's just as *flexible*." Stanley sneers. "If you're trying to get your *dick* wet."

Alex's ears are roaring and his hands feel like they've been dipped into clam chowder. He doesn't respond. He couldn't just punch his asset manager like he had with Baxter, could he?

Stanley continues his Shakespearean villain monologue. "I have you by the balls, Gray. And you're nowhere near fulfilling your sponsorship quota for the fiscal year. You're standing on thin fucking ice. Need I remind you, you would be nothing without me?"

Alex grips the handles of his chair but remains silent. How could he forget?

It's been a few days since she and Alex had their little romp in the hay. Callie is still undecided about how she feels about their reunion. She had tried to cope by swiping on Tinder for a bit, and while it did wonders for her self-confidence, it felt empty and a little like the sensation you get in your stomach after eating a large McDonald's fries in one sitting.

She's closing up shop for the night at the Asana Peace and Serenity studio when she notices a light on in Sandra's back office. She really loves this woman's style. It's eclectic but comforting. The lady sure knows how to place a Himalayan salt lamp.

"Hey, Sandra?" Callie knocks on the door and peeks her head in. "I'm just packing up. You good? It's getting late."

Sandra nods at her, staring off into space. She's wearing a gorgeous green kaftan tonight. A scented candle flickers on her desk and the smell of sandalwood fills the air.

"Sandra, are you alright?" Callie asks, approaching the desk. She'd like to think that as employer and employee, they've reached a point where they can give a shit about each other outside of schedules and payroll. Sometimes it's touch-and-go, especially with Sandra traveling so often for business and pleasure. The woman knows how to work hard to play hard.

"It's my ex-husband." Sandra looks forlorn. The woman pinches the bridge of her nose with a focused exhale. "He's been picked up in Vegas again. He's asking for bail." Well, that escalated.

Callie blinks, unsure of how to respond. "Alex's dad."

"Yes, Alex's father."

Callie looks down at the floor, a crumbling sensation in her chest.

"I can't help him anymore, I'm afraid," Sandra adds. Callie isn't sure who she's talking about here.

The woman's gaze drifts to a family portrait gathering dust in the office's corner. It sits on the edge of a bookshelf, forgotten but still in plain view of the woman's desk chair. A young Alex, with ears the size of saucers, smiles into the camera. A young Sandra with \ stands behind him, her hands on his shoulders. And to her right, the handsome Max Bardot, looking helplessly in love with his wife.

"It'll be alright," Sandra says. Callie tears her eyes away from the portrait to look back at her. "Everything will be alright in the end. If it's not alright, it's not the end."

She's not sure why, but after she locks up at the studio, leaving

Sandra to brood in her office, Callie hightails it over to Alex's gym.

She bangs on the glass door until he comes to fetch her. It was a total crapshoot, guessing he might be there this late, but she has a sinking suspicion he spends an unhealthy amount of time at High Octane Cross Fit. Just a sinking suspicion.

"It's not Tuesday. Or Thursday," he says as he swings the door open. Callie blinks at him, confused. Oh right. Their fuck schedule. For which, uh, they haven't even officially re-activated their subscription. The hookup subscription. To which they both subscribed to. Until a few weeks ago.

"No, fuck, I'm not here for that," she says. He takes in her frenzied state as she pushes past him into the gym.

He grunts.

"Alex, it's your dad," she says, stopping in the center of the gym, near a pile of tires, her hands on her hips.

He makes a sound of annoyance at this. Frustration shrouds him and he crosses his arms. "What's he done now?"

"He's in Vegas needing bail, and your mom can't do it. She needs you, Alex," Callie pleads with him. "I've never seen her like this."

His face darkens in understanding. "Fan of my father's, were you?" He asks her. "Figures." Of course she would be. She's grease-covered and ever so trigger-happy, just like him.

"That's neither here nor there, Alex, and you know it."

"Fuck off, Callie." His voice breaks here. It's a delicate, hoarse thing.

"He needs your help," she tries him again. "I don't understand."

"You wouldn't."

Something is clawing at her throat. "I never even knew *my* parents," she blurts. Play the pity card. Maybe he'll fetch.

He exhales. Her skin now feels like it's vibrating at an incomprehensible decibel. Why can't he understand? She wants to shove him. She wants to punch him.

Instead, she snarls and jumps up at him as tears well up in her eyes. She hits his arms with her palms, making a choked sound.

"Why," she wails, "don't," another smack to his bicep, "you," she kicks him in the shins, "understand?"

He endures this assault for a moment before grabbing her by the shoulders to still her. Instead, they wrestle. Neither of them are MMA masters, either. And while it's not playful, it's not an aggressive thing either.

It's like all this weird pent-up tension they both carry just somehow got channeled into the most bizarre wrestling match ever.

The thing is, this chick could decimate him if she wanted to. If she really wanted to. And he, a Cross Fit instructor who regularly draws blood from his business partner Leon Baxter, could do the same.

Instead, they end up rolling around on the ground like desperate goddamn toddlers fighting over the last good crayon in the coloring box. She pulls at his hair, and he yelps, before rolling on top of her to loom over her. She gets crafty, though, and squirms out from beneath him to crawl over, holding his lower back steady with a strategic knee pressed into his dorsal.

He flips over, and Callie ends up straddling him, sweaty, panting, frustrated.

She remembers fighting a little boy like this when she was younger. The urchin had been on her turf, diving in *her* dumpster. Everyone in a two-mile radius had known the Arby's back alley had been *hers*.

"Stop it!" she screams at him. Her voice reverberates across the otherwise silent gym.

"You stop!" He pushes her up and off him, and she tumbles over to lie beside him. They both pant there, their breathing matched up in a synced tempo. Her hands outstretched, his legs spread-eagled. She looks at the ceiling far above, exposed wiring and pipes snaking across it.

Their breath evens out.

Chapter Nineteen

Minutes pass, maybe hours. She can feel the sound of her heartbeat in her own ears.

"Why did you ghost me?" she whispers. He almost doesn't hear her.

"I don't know," he tells her. It would just be too difficult to explain. Too dumb. She wouldn't understand. She couldn't understand, could she? It's all so *dumb*. It's just his boss and his stupid rules.

He feels ice in his fingertips at the memory of hot, threatening breath over him.

Callie turns her head to face him, her cheek pressed across the cool rubber of the floor. She tries to read his face here, failing miserably. His eyes are still fixed on the ceiling above. She notices the eye twitch again. The one she had thought meant he was shooting up.

"Was it something I did?" she prods.

"No." He shakes his head.

And then: "I missed you, Alex."

He blinks at the ceiling, still unable to look her in the eye. "I was right here." He doesn't know why he says that, but like he was, wasn't he? She could have just come over to the gym if she had wanted, if she had missed him.

Meanwhile, Callie's chest flutters, despite all logic, rhyme, or reason, telling her to drop this dude like a hot goddamn potato. What a clueless fuck-up. The memory of Sandra haunts her, though.

"You can tell me what's up," she tries instead.

He opens his mouth to speak and then closes it.

He swallows. "My mom was constantly traveling for her show," he speaks quickly. "My dad, he was traveling for races, I guess." He pauses and finally turns to meet her gaze. "So, he did this a lot when I was a kid. Got arrested."

They stare at each other. Side by side. On the floor. They're lying on the goddamn floor.

He fish gapes again when she doesn't respond. "I just wanted to move on from all that. Start something new and leave it all behind."

Callie's skin is crawling with an indiscernible sensation. "I have to go," she says, standing up.

He sits up to watch her, resting on his elbows, but remains on the floor.

"Where are you going?"

"I just, I have a late shift at Haven's." She's fucking lying and they both know it. It's the middle of the goddamn night and nobody fixes carburetors at this hour.

Callie makes her way to the bluffs. She hightails it there. She tucks her phone into her sports bra and runs, just runs to the edge of the bluffs and looks down at the ocean hitting the beach. The waves hit the sand forcefully–*swish whoosh swish bam*–unrelenting and violent in the summer night air.

"Breathe, Callie," she tells herself out loud. "Breathe." The full moon illuminates the water, and she stands there, trying to keep her breath even and focused, as more and more constellations reveal themselves across the swath of inky sky above.

After she leaves, Alex sits on the rubber flooring for an hour.

He lies down and closes his eyes, his dark hair fanning out around his head.

She takes some time off mid-week from both the studio and Haven's playing dog mommy for a day. She enjoys parading the labradoodle up and down the city streets. He's so goddamn friendly, and the kids love him.

She's walking him down to the wharf when they run into one Alex Bardot, departing from a fitness gear store downtown. Fuck.

"Hey," Callie greets him as she pulls Kiki tight on the leash to get him to heel.

The dog has other ideas. He recognizes Alex and tugs aggressively, dragging her towards him. Alex stands, stone-faced, as the labradoodle jumps, his paws on Alex's thighs as he pants and slobbers.

"Hey Kiki," Alex mumbles, giving him a half-assed pat on the head.

"I'm watching him for your mom," she explains. "She's out of town."

"Figures," Alex says, passive aggressively. He's doing his best to withstand the friendly onslaught of Kiki's attempts at a slobbery kiss.

She remembers how they had left things that night at the gym, and guilt licks at her.

"Do you? Would you want to? We could go get pizza or something. At the wharf," she meets his eyes, "while I walk Kiki. He looks like he misses you."

Alex casts a glance down at Kiki, who's looking up at him now with excited eyes, tongue lolling out the side of his mouth.

"Sure, I could eat a pizza."

They walk down the main drag, crossing the street to a roundabout with a dolphin fountain in the middle. The pier extends far beyond, deep into the channel. Tall, thin palm trees dot the path leading up to the beach. They've been here before, a while ago, when it wasn't as sunny. Callie feels her thighs clench at the unpleasant memory of a UTI. But now, it's a weekday afternoon and a warm summer day. And there aren't too many tourists around.

They grab two oversized slices of pizza. The cheese is gooey, it's greasy, and exactly what Callie was craving. In retrospect, she was kidding herself, thinking she could survive on a paleo diet. She's not a cave woman.

Callie and Alex walk with Kiki to the far end of the pier and settle in on a picnic bench overlooking the channel. The faint shape of islands in the distance paints the horizon.

"How's work?" she asks.

He shrugs. "Fine."

Ugh, he is horrible at casual conversation. She had to wrestle some deep shit out of him last time, and she supposes that's only the tip of the iceberg.

"Do you have any friends, Alex?" she blurts out. Where the fuck did that come from?

He looks taken aback. "Sure, I have friends." He has Baxter, right? That counts. They have banter in their shared office space. That's legitimate. Plus, he has a lot of followers on Instagram who adore his pectorals *and* his dedication to a healthy lifestyle. He shoves another bite of pizza down his throat.

"You do?"

"I do."

She's skeptical as all hell. "Name a friend."

He blinks. He can't *actually* say Baxter. Instead, the words leave his mouth before he can stop them: "I have you."

"Alex." She laughs at him, she fucking laughs in his face. Maybe the laughing was mean, but come on, is this guy kidding himself?

"What?"

Oh, he is kidding himself.

He's quiet now, the cogs turning in his head. This is all the stuff he doesn't like to think about. He doesn't need friends because he's always had the comfort of the gym to fall back on. The rush there. He gets a minimum amount of social interaction from the classes he teaches at High Octane. And he's doing just fine!

He slumps his shoulders a bit in frustration. He wants to squirm away from the situation, maybe he can make up a half-assed excuse like *she* did last time, but then Callie turns to feed Kiki a piece of pepperoni and he sees the wisps of hair at the back of her neck. She's wearing it in a ponytail today.

"When's your birthday?" he asks her as he bites into his own slice of pizza.

"Why?" She turns back to look at him as Kiki licks grease off her fingers.

"I don't know. Isn't that a friendly thing to know?" He's struggling with his pizza now. The cheese is doing the melty thing where it connects to the body of the pizza but is also attached to the part he has in his mouth. She suppresses a giggle. She's become slightly wary about his ability to handle a jumbo slice.

She holds her own slice up to her mouth, taking a confident bite into the crust. "I guess. But I don't know," she tells him.

He looks at her. He has his own reservations about *her* pizza-eating skills. Is she eating it backwards? "You don't know what?"

"I don't know my birthday," she repeats. She doesn't want to explain this to anyone again. It's a fucking plague. Every job application, every coworker asking when they should get her a gift, yadda yadda. "I was born in the winter."

Thankfully, he senses her unease and drops the subject. They finish their pizza and make their way down to the beach. They don't speak, but he puts down his hoodie on the sand so they can both sit on it. Their knees touch as they watch Kiki chase after seagulls.

As the high noon sun dips lower in the sky, she feels herself grow warm and sleepy. She dozes off for a bit until sleep overtakes her and she falls into a midday nap.

When she wakes, she's curled up on top of Alex's hoodie. She looks around for him. The sun is now hanging low over the horizon.

She then spots two figures down by the surf. A man and a dog.

It's Alex, playing with Kiki. He's throwing a stick, the elderly dog hobbling over to pick it up in his mouth and stumble back towards Alex.

Callie covers her forehead from the glare of the sunset to watch this for a moment.

As she watches this scene, it feels like she's intruding on something secret. Like she's a voyeur to something special. There's a smile on Alex's face she's never seen before. His face is relaxed as he plays with the labradoodle. He gets to his knees to mess with the dog's ears, speaking to him in an excited voice.

A grin spreads across Callie's own face. So like, she knew this guy wasn't all fucking muscle and hard edges. She's always known, maybe. This is a side of him she's never had the privilege of seeing. She thinks could get used to it.

Chapter Twenty

The next day, on a whim, Callie enters *"Stanley HIGH OCTANE management"* into Google, the inquiry based on Alex's Instagram page. The email there is listed as stanley@highoctane.net).

Unfortunately, there's nothing concrete or official-looking available. Not even a website. But she does find a Reddit thread from a Los Angeles-based user:

"This dude is the worst. He's a fucking con artist and drug pusher" *"Gives you a cushy deal and signs you into a legally binding hellhole,"*
"Am still in debt from lawyer fees to get out of this thing."
"Ruined my life.
"He's a horrible manager and travels around the US taking advantage of young talent and sucking the life out of them" *"Stay away from this dude!!!"*
"Influencers beware!"

Callie had her suspicions about Alex's manager. Mostly based on short, tense conversations with Alex himself. But until now, she'd never had reason or motivation to look into the guy's life like this. Who cared if he had a shitty boss? Now, she supposes., she did.

At first, she thought it was funny. But maybe there was more to the dumb app and Alex's situation than she had realized. Still, she supposes, it didn't excuse his behavior. She clicks out of the Reddit page and the browser, more confused than when she had first opened Google.

She had something else to do.

Callie has been on hold with the human services of Santa Fe County for an hour now. They keep answering, trying to push her off to other office workers, transferring her, and then turning shitty jazz music on in her ear.

"Yes, hi, I'm case number 52558. I'm just trying to follow-up on my inquiry, and I haven't heard anything in nearly two weeks."

"You moved away, ma'am. Your last address on file was a return to sender."

"No, I know, but I was told I could continue the search from out of state. I submitted my address change."

"We don't have any new information for you, not since we sent over the death certificates."

"The what?" Callie's voice catches in her throat. She's at Haven's right now, and steadies herself by gripping her workbench.

"We sent you copies of the death certificates, based on your disclosure search?"

"No, I don't know what you're talking about."

"Sorry, ma'am." The office worker pauses, and Callie hears the click-clacking of a keyboard. "Oh, they appear to have been returned to the sender. To us, that is."

Callie presses end on the call. She had begun this search ages ago, with next to nothing to go on. But it appears the bureaucracy had been working on her inquiry, long after she had departed the desert she once called home. And now...

She pauses, blinking back tears. She picks her phone back up, tentatively scrolling through her contacts. Her thumb hovers, trembling, before it makes its decision.

Callie: Can I come over

The typing speech bubble appears for forty-five seconds. She counts it, holding her breath.

Cross Fit, Rock Hard Abs: Sure
Cross Fit, Rock Hard Abs: [CURRENT LOCATION SENT]

She bikes over to the pinned location on the map, hooking her bike up to a street sign near the towering luxury high-rise. The grand apartment building has a lot of modern art and sculptures. The minute she sees him in the lobby, the tension in her shoulders is gone. She lets out a deep breath and gives him a look.

"Can we just hang out for a sec?" she asks as he approaches her.

"Like?"

"Literally, just hang out."

He looks her over. "Of course."

She follows him into an opulent elevator, and they stand an awkward distance apart.

"How's Kiki?" he asks her, pressing his floor number on the illuminated keypad.

"He's back with Sandra." She notes how he prefers to ask about the dog, not his father. Max, as far as she knew, was still holed up in a Las Vegas jail.

They don't speak until they get up to his apartment.

He opens the door, wooden and painted a glossy black, adorned with a silver minimalist knocker.

"Do you want a coffee or something?" he asks her as they walk through the entryway into the kitchen.

"Do you have any barley grass?" she tries to joke, and he gives her a sideways glare.

He opens his fridge and places two cans of La Croix on the granite counter, one lemon, and one pomelo. She grabs the lemon like a self-respecting human would.

"What's going on?" he asks her as he snaps open the other can.

She breathes in, she breathes out. She settles on one of the leather barstools at the kitchen island and takes a sip of the carbonated beverage. "Have you ever done something knowing it would fuck you up, but you did it, anyway?"

He stares at her. Of course he fucking has. She knows he has. He's, uh, done her.

"Yeah," he says.

"I did one of those things today and I just. Didn't want to be alone," her voice trails off, "so..."

He watches her curl in on herself, sipping at her La Croix.

He blurts out, "You want to watch a movie?"

She looks up at him, a bit surprised. Initially, her reaction is coiled frustration in the pit of her stomach. And then, she realizes, she wants nothing more than to sit on the couch with this guy and just watch a fucking movie.

So they settle in on his black leather couch. He hands her a blanket, and she wraps it around her shoulders as he scrolls through the Netflix options, hesitating. He knows exactly what he used to watch when he was younger, when he felt like this, the way she does now. And she doesn't say a word when he flicks over to his selection: *Contact*, starring Jodie Foster.

"I watched this a lot as a kid," he explains to her. "It's one of my favorites."

She looks up at him with a smile and moves over so that her knees settle on his lap. He rests his hand where their legs are touching, and presses play.

After the movie, he has her tucked into his chest, her head curled up under his chin so that she's breathing into his collarbone.

"What did you think?" he asks her, staying still, terrified of shattering whatever trance they're both in right now.

"I liked it." She tilts her head up a bit so she can look at him. "Are wormholes like that real, do you think?"

"Could be," he shrugs. She's opening the can of worms here that's his interest in these topics. "There are lots of theories on how they'd work. You can consider string theory. There are even theories of parallel universes." Oh fuck, he's realizing he let his guard down here, the words are just pouring out of him—she's going to think –

"So this stuff interests you?" she says. She curls herself closer to him, if that were possible.

"Oh, yeah. First, I was just interested in aliens," he motions to the movie, where the credits are now playing, "but then I started reading about the theory of astrophysics."

Shut up! Shut up! Shut up!

"You said something about parallel universes?" she wonders out loud.

Is there a universe where her parents are alive, and they kept her, maybe?

He nods. "Just a theory. Maybe there are many versions of us, but maybe there are universes based on the choices we make. They create different timelines and stuff." She doesn't want to hear about multiverse, what is he doing? Why can't he stop?

"And the choices other people make," she adds. "I think I get it."

"Though I'd like to think," he murmurs into her hair, which smells like grapefruit and sandalwood, "if that's the case, in every universe, people are unstoppable forces." He pauses, tracing a pattern on her elbow. "We will always find a way to collide with each other."

"In every universe?"

"Yes, in every universe," he smiles down at her. "With the

multiple universes, you know. Different versions of us. Maybe there's a version of me out there. That's not a fuck up."

"Maybe there's one where you're even worse," she giggles. She's noticing a recurring theme here. He had mentioned a Carl Sagan when they had first fucked. Now aliens, multiple universes, yadda yadda. She doesn't hate it.

He laughs with her, vibrations in his chest. "Do you believe in that? I could be worse?" he asks. His voice cracks a little.

"I believe that we are who we are. But, I guess, sometimes, there's stuff out of our control," she whispers. She thinks about the Reddit thread on his boss.

"And that stuff affects us?"

Callie thinks about that as she separates herself from their embrace and stretches out her limbs. "I think we have a choice in how it affects us. So yes, our choices make us who we are. And no, we can't always control what happens to us."

"That's fucking cryptic, Callie," he says, leaning back against the couch. He realizes he misses the warmth and shape of her. Now that she's pulled away from him to stretch, he's getting the same feeling he gets when he loses a sock in the laundry.

"I never said I had all the answers."

Chapter Twenty-One

Callie slips out in the early hours of the morning, right as the night sky is becoming a gradual gradient of light blue to ink.

After finishing the movie and talking for a bit, they had fallen asleep on his couch, their limbs twisted together like tangled headphones. You know how hard it is to undo a pair of tangled headphones? Fuck that.

She woke up, enveloped by his form, his magnetic, solid form, all muscle and warmth. He also somehow still smelled incredible first thing in the morning. If she could just cover herself with him, shield herself from reality and spend the day drifting in and out of sleep, in and out of each other, even but these thoughts were likely all hazy, sleep-drunk feelings.

This was all before she had woken up, before she could process the events of yesterday. What had led her here, to Alex Bardot's arms.

She had felt the sound of his heartbeat roaring in her ears. Erratic, even in his sleep. She separated herself from him and tiptoed out of his apartment.

She decided that, because they hadn't fucked, it wasn't that bad, because like, it wasn't a one-night stand, and they weren't even dating, and...? She can sneak out at like 5am and it's fine, right?

Right? It wasn't that bad. They didn't owe each other anything. This was fine.

So now she wanders back down to the beach, where she had been only last week with Alex, where she had watched him play fetch with Kiki. She stands by the water, letting the chilly surf cover her toes. This usually did the trick for her.

She was alone, trying to cope with the sensation of wanting to cry, with her toes in the water. Trying to process. Properly process the search for her family coming to an end. A dead end. The finality of this. The truth she had kept shielded from herself for so long.

She says it out loud: "They're really dead." A heavy sigh. She feels like it might come from someone else standing next to her. She flexes her hand slightly, as if she could grasp the hand of that phantom, someone standing by her side.

"But you always knew that, didn't you?" she whispers to herself again, when the phantom hand does not appear.

She looks out to the horizon where the rising sun from the east is casting a glow across the water, and the foggy, vague shape and outlines of the channel islands in the distance begin to incrementally reveal themselves.

She walks along the surf, sandals in one hand, swinging them slightly as she leaves footprints behind her that get erased every time the water drifts back in to meet her toes.

"They're dead and they didn't want you," she says out loud to herself, almost sing-songy.

Why aren't the tears coming? Can she *taunt* herself into crying? That sounds healthy, right?

She looks like she's lost it, talking to herself at dawn down by the beach. If pelicans could talk.

There's that emptiness in her chest again. It feels fucking endless, holy shit, talk about a void! She feels like even if she ever found a way to fill it she would scoop whatever it was she needed or wanted into a container that would just drain it right back out.

Like a hole you dig in the sand to collect water around your sandcastle but when you fill it, the water dissipates through the sand and you're left with a damp but empty trough you worked much too hard on and a castle left unprotected by an empty moat? And ugh, why won't the water just *stay put*?

"They're dead and they didn't want you!" She's laughing out loud now. She's trying to laugh it off and instead makes weird gross choking sounds and she throws her sandals up onto the beach, away from the surf. A perturbed pelican is startled and flies away, giving her a dirty look.

Callie retrieves her sandals, but ends up walking home barefoot.

After she gets back to the cottage, she spends a few minutes picking little rocks out from where they've embedded themselves in the bottoms of her feet.

She knocks on Dean's bedroom door, and pushes it open to peer in. When she sees that he's still in bed, she crawls in under the covers next to him.

He sleepily loops a hand over her shoulders and pulls her in close.

She wants to cry in somebody's arms right now. And even with her best friend right here, holding her, something just doesn't feel right. It's not that he isn't comforting, it's just that the puzzle pieces don't quite match up in the way she'd hoped they would, maybe.

"What's up?" he mumbles.

She scrunches up her eyes and nose and exhales as she feels the bricks and barriers and blinds building up and shuttering around those very secret dark places inside of her and it's like she can *hear* herself just shutting down. The barriers are up. For now. Deep insightful sharing session is NOT a go.

"Bad night," she finally replies. The tears will not come, not just yet, maybe.

Still, the comfort. She nuzzles into him and breathes in her best friend and roommate, comforted by the mere presence of another human being. Particularly one who, without rhyme or reason in her opinion, appears to care about her.

"Love you," she whispers to Dean. The two words come slowly.

"Love you too," he whispers back, his words coming easily, and he presses a soft kiss to her hairline.

She stays there, suspended in the cocoon of his familiar presence, until she hears his breath even out again as he falls back asleep.

Callie, unfortunately, stays awake for a long while, closing her eyes and watching the kaleidoscope of shapes and colors and bright spots on the back of her eyelids as she listens to Dean's even breathing.

Chapter Twenty-Two

Alex Bardot is no stranger to nightmares, and they get downright Freudian sometimes.

We get it, Freud was a douche bag and like, let's not take a lot of what he says to heart, but sometimes Alex's dreams hit shit a little too on the nose.

He still gets nightmares with zero chill about things he thought were long gone from the neural pathways of his brain.

Like the kids on the playground, locking him outside after recess. He had gotten in so much trouble, accused of skipping class. In reality, he just couldn't get back into the school through any of the locked doors.

He could still see their faces pressed against the window, laughing at him. They taunted him. He had big ears; you see. That was a popular jab. And he read a lot too; that was another. He didn't understand the cruelty of children, even as he had gotten older. Children like to have someone to exclude, maybe to feel better about themselves. Maybe because their parents worked busy jobs and didn't read them bedtime stories. Or something.

Any way.

Now that he's older, he has a similar nightmare, but in a different form.

Tonight, he's chasing someone—he can't see all of her face but she's got a funny hairstyle and she's laughing, beckoning him to follow her—down a dark hallway, and she turns and she shuts the door on him and he can hear laughter from the other side. Familiar laughter. He grasps at this thought, but it turns into desert sand that falls through his fingers, despite his clenched fist. He's banging on the door until his knuckles turn raw and bleed. The door melts into the wall and disappears.

But then Alex feels something else. Hot, swampy breath on the back of his neck that makes the ends of his hair flutter slightly with each exhale. He turns slowly to look behind him, and sees a tall, dark, thin, wrinkled man holding out a palm. As Alex looks down into the outstretched hand of the man, old and gnarled with knobby knuckles and claw-like fingers, he sees what's held there and he feels the wind knocked out of him. The next thing he knows, he's falling down. He's falling and falling and falling.

And he wakes up in a cold sweat, his heart trying to beat its way out of his chest.

But he can't move.

He can't move a muscle, but he's awake and he's yelling, isn't he? Where are the sounds?

He's yelling, and he swears he can move his arms. He thinks he's moving his arms isn't he moving isn't he –

He hears laughter again. It's a low nightmarish chuckle.

He shuts his eyes and feels his heartbeat, and waits. He waits because it can't last forever . . . can it? There's a very distinct sensation that someone, or something, is sitting on his chest.

When he does—when he wakes up, and his nervous system activates out of that particularly nasty REM cycle, he throws himself to the ground next to his couch, heaving.

He stays there, on his hands and knees, relishing the feeling of being able to move his fucking body. He clenches his fists slightly, and flexes the corded muscles, feeling them ripple across his form. It's delicious.

He can move. He's not paralyzed. He gasps for breath, even though he's been asleep, technically. This whole time.

A thought comes to mind.

"Callie?" he asks the floor beneath him. "Callie?" His voice rises slightly, echoing throughout his empty living room.

Alex stumbles around his apartment and it feels like they have filled his head with swamp sludge. He feels pounding in his ears and his eyes hurt like a frat party hangover.

"Callie?" He asks again tentatively, stumbling into his kitchen, his bedroom. Where is she?

It takes a moment before he realizes–she's gone. She left.

Alex stands in the middle of his empty apartment, stunned, for a long moment before he's able to move again. In some animal part of his hindbrain, he wonders if he's paralyzed again, if this is some extended nightmare you think you've woken from when really you're still trapped in it.

But it's no dream. She left before he woke.

He stumbles into his bathroom, into the shower, and he turns on the water.

Standing for thirty minutes under the cold water until his tunnel vision dissolves and the sensation of someone sitting on his chest slowly lifts.

He thinks he might be crying, but there's too much water on his face from the showerhead, so he can't be sure.

Callie finally wakes up in Dean's bed hours later to the smell of breakfast cooking and coffee brewing.

Dean is gone, however, and she stumbles into their shared kitchen to see him standing with Penn at his back, nuzzling at each other. Rita is nowhere to be seen. Callie should inquire about that ongoing drama. She can't keep track of who's fucking whom.

Penn turns when he hears her enter and chuckles. "There was a gremlin in bed with my boyfriend this morning."

She grins at him, squinting her eyes a bit, and settles herself into one of the thrifted wicker chairs they use at their kitchen table.

"The gremlin wants pancakes." Her voice sounds hoarse and her eyes feel groggy, even though she hadn't been crying. At all.

"Chocolate chip or blueberry?" Dean peers over at her.

"Both," she blurts. She's starving. She wasn't sure when her last meal had been. Maybe the La Croix at Alex's house yesterday.

Penn comes over and runs his hand over the top of her head in a soothing gesture. "Everything okay, sunshine?"

"No," she tells him with a groan. "But it will be," she adds.

He kisses the top of her scalp. "That's what I like to hear. Everything will be okay in the end."

"If it's not okay, it's not the end?" she muses back at him with a smile. Looks like Sandra was copiously peppering her wisdom around the studio.

"Precisely," he tells her with a wink and a shoot of his finger guns.

She shoos Penn away as Dean comes over to the kitchen table with a plate of pancakes.

She dives in, starving, and inhales her food with large bites. The pancakes are comforting, and she can feel her blood sugar levels rise. She's less grumpy after a few swallows. And while chocolate chip pancakes don't fill the existential void you get from discovering the parents who abandoned you are dead and gone, they don't necessarily *hurt*, either. After all, they're pancakes.

As her belly fills and her chewing slows, she watches the way Penn and Dean caress each other. Penn kisses Dean's neck where it meets his shoulder. The way they playfully bump hips together. The way they hum together, both slightly out of tune. The small things.

And for a moment, against her better judgment, her mind drifts back to the way she had woken up in someone's arms that morning. The way she had run to that someone yesterday after all that shit had gone down with social services, how he had let her into his apartment with open arms. How he didn't ask her exactly what had happened, or why she had texted him when she did, but he just knew to watch a movie with her at that precise moment. A small thing.

She then physically shakes her head out of that, because, well, she could swear she had felt a tear begin to form at the inner corner of one of her eyes.

After she's done eating, her attention span returning, Callie notices an envelope on the kitchen table. The sender is the California Department of Education.

She lets out a small yelp.

Dean and Penn look at her with knowing smiles.

A week ago, she had sat down to take the test and conveniently pushed it to the back of her mind. Dog sitting distracted her at work, at the auto shop. She didn't want to get her hopes up. See, she knew all about the dangers of getting her hopes up.

"Is that–" she says.

"Yep." Penn's looking at her with a shit-eating grin.

"When did it come in?"

"Yesterday afternoon."

She scrambles, tearing open the results of her GED test, and stares down at the score.

Her mind wanders back to when she had first endeavored on this journey, and the number of times she'd read up on how to do this and studied whilst Alex Bardot fucked her into oblivion. How she would scroll on her smart phone with his dick balls deep inside of her.

Well. That had been a life choice.

"How did you do?" Penn asks her, sipping coffee.

She looks up at them. "197." A life choice that had somehow worked out for her.

"That's good, right?"

She smiles. "It's really good, you guys."

She's momentarily distracted from the sadness, and something else creeps in at the edges. Something lighter. Because this is it. Her story is about to begin. The one she always felt was just out of reach. Maybe it's about to begin.

She gets up and dances around the kitchen table. Penn joins her, placing his hands on her hips, then Dean stands and places his hands on Penn's, and soon enough they're all bunny hopping around the kitchen while the smell of burning bacon fills the small space.

Chapter Twenty-Three

The next day, Ax Gray distracts himself by responding to several Instagram direct messages. A couple of thirsty fans are asking him for shirtless photos, and he obliges, posing in the bathroom mirror and flexing.

Unfortunately, it all feels very hollow and distinctly not thrilling. Well, not as thrilling as it used to be. Maybe they're all lovely people. He's sure they are. But the influx of notifications makes the back of his neck itch, so he logs out of his account, wanders back into the gym office and puts his phone away, tucking it into one of his desk drawers.

Later, as he's sweating on a rowing machine, he notices Stanley watching him from a corner of the gym, his arms crossed over his chest. He approaches Ax as he exerts himself further with each row.

Stanley points at the younger man's abdomen.

"What's that?"

Alex looks down, stopping his relentless assault on the machine. "The Adidas shorts?"

"No." Stanley leans over to Ax's still form and squeezes a small amount of skin that's spilling over the top of his shorts. Ax recoils away from the touch, loses his balance, and falls from his seat to the floor.

He breathes, looking up at Stanley, whose face is poised with mirth.

"What's your percentage at, young man?"

"Eight percent," Ax sputters out in reply. He had measured last week.

"Hmm, I don't think so. What are we going to do about that?" Stanley shakes his head, clicks his tongue and saunters away.

Alex feels like his head is spinning. He looks down at the skin protruding over the top of his shorts. It's skin, it's just skin. So what is this guy playing at?

But there's a lurch in his stomach and he's not certain of the source. Stanley's touch, that wicked grin? Maybe he just overexerted himself on the rowing machine.

But maybe it's the thought of him losing control of the one thing he's always kept in check. Could that make the room spin? Who knows? What was it he kept in check, again? He can't think straight.

He grabs a towel and races out into the relative privacy of the back alleyway behind the gym. Seconds later, he's gagging into the space near the dumpster until there's nothing but acid coming up the back of his throat.

Cross Fit, Rock Hard Abs: u up?
Callie: yeah
Cross Fit, Rock Hard Abs: dtf?

Callie stares at her phone, blinking. It had been a couple days since they had watched a movie on his couch and things had gotten particularly . . . cuddly. She also hadn't texted him after she snuck out before dawn. But again, that was all fine.

She shrugs to herself. Why not?

Callie: meet me at Haven's

Haven's is neutral ground.
Anyway. She gets on her bike and rides to the garage.
The shop is dark and empty this late at night, and when he arrives he walks with her into the lit repair bay.
They kiss. She runs his hands up his back, down the front of his abdomen.
He swats her hands away when they trail over his stomach. His breathing gets ragged.
She mistakes this for arousal.
After they kiss a while longer, Callie presses her hand against the front of his shorts for the familiar feeling of hardened flesh, and . . . oh. Uh.
Their eyes meet and before he looks away from her, a red flush forms across his cheeks. She can't read whatever is behind those eyes. But she knows it's nothing good.
"I can help–" she offers.
She positions him up against an SUV she'd been working on earlier and gets on her knees in front of him. The concrete is cold and hard, but it makes her feel grounded despite the strange energy between them.
After a few minutes of some very enthusiastic work on her end, things just aren't happening. She's tonguing his balls, for fuck's sake.
Callie straightens, getting up off the floor and brushing off her knees. She tilts her head to try to meet his gaze as she pulls his Adidas shorts back up around his hips, tucking him away.
She kisses his jaw line, but he can't meet her eyes. He just can't look at her.
She closes the inches of space between them and lays her head on his chest, breathing, listening to how fast his heartbeat is beneath his pectorals and his rib cage. He makes a sound that's

almost like a sob, but maybe it's a cough, maybe he's choking on his own spit. That happens.

Then she feels his hands creep towards the waistband of her jeans, and she grabs his wrist to stop him. Callie brings his hand, Alex's huge hand, up to her mouth, and she presses a quick kiss to the space between his thumb and index finger.

"Maybe another night," she whispers, breaking the silence that had built up between them like so many layers of dust. Her breath against the rough skin of his hand meddling with that dust.

He says nothing back, and as he pushes her away, nodding, she swears she sees tears in his eyes, but maybe they're just glistening more than usual.

He gives her a mumble of "I'll text you," as he hightails it out of the garage, still unable to look her in the eye, stomping away and pulling on his sweatshirt.

Chapter Twenty-Four

The guilt licks at her the next day, and after teaching a class at the studio, Callie wanders over to High Octane Cross Fit unannounced. She expects to find Alex there, alone, as per usual, but after she steps inside the gym, she's accosted by an old white man. His mere appearance makes her feel misandristic.

"Ah, I've heard so much about you, Miss Callie," the old wrinkled sketchy dude says as he slithers up to her and licks his lips.

She steps back. "God, I hope not," she retorts. She puts two and two together. This must be Stanley.

"Have you ever considered professional management in your athletic endeavors?" His eyes travel up and down her body in a very obvious way. She wants to be wearing a black trash bag right now, stat. Also, who the fuck starts a conversation like this? If you could call this a conversation.

"Athletic endeavors?" she asks, with a chuckle. Her gaze drifts to the back of the gym, to the doors leading to the locker room and office, as she looks for Alex.

"Yes, professional sponsorships. Modeling opportunities. Photoshoots?"

"I'm just a yoga instructor, my dude."

"You'd be surprised what a fit young thing like you can make online these days. The sponsors love a body like yours," his voice drops. His hands encircle her biceps, and almost as soon as his clammy gross flesh contacts her skin, she pries it off and holds his wrist in a vice grip that makes him wince.

"Don't touch me," she snarls. "Don't you dare fucking do that again."

He's almost whimpering now, under the strength of her grip, and she pushes him away from her with fervor. He stumbles back, rubbing his wrist with a dark snicker.

"I like your spunk," he says.

"You won't like it when it knocks your teeth out, old man," she growls at him.

She sees Alex appear at the far end of the gym, poking his head out from the office door. Finally.

He approaches Stanley and Callie, storming up to them. If she didn't know any better, she'd say he looked like a mother bear whose cub had just been fucked with.

"What's going on here?" he inquires, his voice sharp with suspicion.

"Just getting to know your little friend," Stanley says with a smile. "She's incredibly charming."

"You're damn right I am," she spits, vitriol dripping from her words and filling the space between the trio.

A pause extends between them all, and Stanley flicks his eyes between Alex and Callie suspiciously.

"I have your food delivery in the back room." Alex meets Callie's eyes here.

She pauses, opening her mouth to speak in confusion–she had canceled that dumb food subscription service ages ago. But then she understands.

"Right, right," she agrees with him. "Better go pick that up."

Alex directs her towards the office by the small of her back, and thankfully, Stanley stays behind, watching them walk away with a scowl.

"Why the fuck is that guy hanging out here?" she whispers when they get to the office.

"He's my manager," he explains.

"I figured, but he's creepy as all hell. I'd rather let a scorpion in my sleeping bag than talk to him again."

Alex shrugs. They stand still in the office, because there's not any food delivery available for pickup.

She taps her foot. "I'm sorry I didn't text you back after we watched the movie."

He snaps his eyes up to meet hers.

"And I'm sorry I snuck out in the morning," she adds. She watches as the lid under his left eye twitches, involuntarily.

He nods. "It's whatever."

Another awkward pause. Ugh, this was that awkward negotiation thing she had been trying to avoid.

"Alex, last night."

He shakes his head. "Don't, please don't."

"Alex, I don't care that you couldn't get it up." The space between them is closed. Even though she is barely able to cover any surface area, she takes his large hands in hers. She clasps them to her chest. "I really don't. It's okay."

He relaxes into her touch and brings his eyes down to where their hands feel like they're melding together.

"Thank you," he says.

"You know how I came to you that afternoon, and we watched a movie?"

He nods.

"You can," she exhales, trying to figure out how to communicate what she's trying to say. "I mean–I can be that for you, if you need."

His eyes drift up from where they're locked on their hands, and he meets her eyes again.

He wants to figure out what kind of star she would be. It is possible that she is a red giant, hot and burning and bright, and has overtaken everything in her path. Maybe she's not a star at all, but she's a constellation, guiding sailors home in the middle of the night. She might be a whole goddamn galaxy.

"I don't do this thing very well," he finally tells her.

She chuckles. "What?"

"Talking."

"I know."

"But I think you've made me realize there's something I have to do. But maybe, I think, I need to do it myself."

She releases his hands and nods.

She departs the office, and he watches the way her ponytail bobs, revealing the hair at the nape.

Callie gives Stanley a dirty look before exiting.

It takes him a few days to get the courage to do it, but his thumb finds its way to the Instagram app on his phone, and over to the "delete account" button.

He deletes Ax Gray's account and then the rest. He sits back in his office chair, hooking his hands behind his head, and waits for it.

Not minutes later, the office door bursts open.

"What did you do, you little shit?" Stanley is seething, his thumbs flying across his iPhone. "Your sponsors are blowing up my inbox."

"I'm done," he whispers, looking up at Stanley and meeting his eyes with a fixed, expressionless gaze.

"No, you're not. I'm getting on the phone with Instagram right now, and we are restoring that account."

"Sue me. I'm done."

His brain reels, remembering the clauses and the fine print in all the contracts he had signed, years ago, all the legal jargon he hadn't bothered to worry about because he'd been young and eager and aimless.

But now he knows, aimless is better than whatever this bullshit he's been doing for the past few years. And the rest of the shit? He'll have to deal with that when it hits the fan. Maybe not right now.

Alex rushes out the front door of High Octane Cross Fit, and runs.

He feels acid in his chest. He runs down towards the wharf.

He runs until he feels his vision cloud at the edges, which happens sometimes, like whatever. It's probably nothing.

He runs down the beach. His pace quickens. It's punishing, and he's sprinting. Maybe he could try track next. He could be a marathoner. He could be anything.

Alex remembers the last time he was here, with her, he remembers, he sees the dolphin fountain in the far distance, back the way he came, but then the dolphin fountain dips and twists and turns into what appears to be sand and surf and more sand –

Falling is a funny thing. Especially when you fall in dreams. In reality, it's much faster, and if you're not expecting it, and not in your right mind, there's fuck all you can do about it.

So, the last thought he has is something along the lines of: *Ouch.*

Chapter Twenty-Five

His heartbeat is no longer erratic. It's a beautiful, even tempo. It's not the frantic arrhythmia she knew so well. She knows this, because she can hear it beeping on a monitor. A monitor hooked up to his chest.

"You had me as your emergency contact."

He hears her voice before he sees her. His throat is dry, and he tries to swallow a few times before speaking.

"It just prompts you to enter one on a new phone. I had broken it again," he mumbles, intent on preserving his pride here. He doesn't even know what's going on, but god forbid this voice thinks there's any sentiment attached to the whole emergency contact thing. *Her* voice, oh right. God forbid.

Meanwhile, Callie considers the fact that he had her cell phone number memorized to where he had typed it in as his emergency contact. But from an outside perspective, that's the last thing he has to be self-conscious of right now.

Alex turns his head. He's lying down. His arms, chest and legs hurt. He'd be more eloquent, but everything hurts.

He feels his brow furrow, he's squinting now. The light, wherever they are, is so fucking bright. It's downright bizarre. He knows he's laying down, but everything is spinning. He can't see everything, but he's sure it's spinning. The right side of his face is numb. He feels a bandage on his cheek, but his arms are too heavy to lift to his face.

What? What's happening? Wait.

He's trying to open his eyes, but it's like there are weights pulling down on them. When he manages to sneak a peek beneath his eyelids, everything comes in blurry. But he sees the shape of her by his bedside. Her.

He squints again, trying to find her in the haze.

"Callie, I–" he says.

"Doping, Alex? That's what you've been doing? Your temper? Your weird mood swings?" She's making a shitty attempt at a level voice, and there's acid fury dripping in her tone. "Of course there wouldn't have been needle marks," she says, but she's talking to herself now, reasoning with the situation. "I knew it. There was something I missed.

"I don't–I," he's grasping at the tightrope of reality, like he has been for some time now. A gust has come and knocked him off and he's clinging by one hand, and there's nothing beneath him. Absolutely nothing. This is it.

"They found fucking *steroids* all over your blood work, you complete moron. What were you thinking? Who do you think you are? Some fucking Olympian? Jesus."

"I couldn't, I didn't -" His words are slurring again. He can't form a coherent thought. He's grasping at the edges, grasping at existence. The bed is shifting beneath him.

"If you're going to say you didn't have a choice, I'm punching you and putting you back into cardiac arrest. I don't give a shit. This is such goddamn bullshit."

Back into cardiac arrest? What? He groans, because everything feels like cement and syrup and he wants to speak, but words, like everything else, are just out of reach.

"They've got you sedated," she says, her voice softening now.

He drifts off again, and she remains at his bedside, curled up in the uncomfortable blue pleather hospital chair.

His drug-induced fever dreams take him down an unwelcome path through memory lane.

When Alex had been a teenager, his parents had sent him away to stay with his weird hippie uncle. He had a "sanctuary" or whatever in the mountains. One of those new age mindfulness centers, you know? This was back before Asana Peace and Serenity studio, of course. His uncle drank weird juices and sat on a pillow doing a lot of deep breathing. For a fifteen-year-old kid into Nightwish and Kurt Cobain, this had been torture.

When things go wrong, we take a few steps back because we don't know what just happened. Because his psyche desperately wants to know where it all went wrong.

But finding out what went wrong isn't always easy. It's difficult to identify.

It's gradual. Like when we continue to put off doing laundry. Until that becomes a habit. When we say one glass of wine, and then it becomes two, and then you're drinking a bottle every night after work and it's tough to stop when you don't precisely know when you even began. When you first turn down a friend's invitation to hang out, and the excuses become easier until they're no longer inviting you to hang out.

When you joke and act like everything is normal, and learn to put up a front and be another person and just survive. Until the shitty foundations you've built shatter, and you realize you were standing on pretty thin ice the whole time and then you're underwater and trapped under the surface. What a nightmare.

So anyway, his parents had sent him away because he was rowdy in school. Throwing temper tantrums, struggling in class. He was smart. Sharp, the teachers would say. Analytical. Carefully chosen words to mask their confusion at his shitty test scores and inability to "Play Well With Others."

But like, his hippie uncle didn't know what the fuck to do with him either. Uncle Dave had gotten increasingly frustrated and annoyed with him. The zen he carried with him crumbled like a poorly made apple pie as he tried to deal with a petulant hormonal teenager coping with an unstable home life and a pair of divorced parents.

There aren't villains in reality. People will fuck you over, yes. You can get fucked over by divorced parents and weird hippie uncles and gross employers, sure. But there's nobody in a castle with magic powers and flying goblins or gargoyles. That's all fantasy.

I mean granted, there's politicians and lawyers. But let's leave them out of this analogy for now.

So you can't blame everything on Ursula, you see? Nobody's here to steal your voice. Except maybe you.

Again, choo choo and all aboard the train of self-pity and privileged white guys and their problems, but here we are.

So where did it all go wrong?

He feels like he's walking through the museum of his life and he keeps turning corners and there's no answer. Alex keeps getting lost. He's looking for a relic that doesn't exist. Instead, his mind descends on a memory. Not a particularly significant memory, but just a memory.

His mother is on a break from her television show, taking him down to the racetrack one weekend. She holds him up on her lap. His kid arms are outstretched, reaching for the race car rounding the track in the distance. His mom gives him a hat with BARDOT emblazoned on it, too big for his toddler head. He giggles and wails. He remembers how wide her smile had been, he remembers how she clutched him close to her chest as she carried him down the precariously tall bleachers towards the race track.

The memory fades away as his mother approaches the race car, and a figure emerges from the driver's seat.

Chapter Twenty-Six

Alex comes to in the early hours of the morning. The physicians haven't even begun their rounds just yet.

A nurse is tending to him at his bedside, making a note of his vitals on a clipboard.

He then notices the warmth of another human body curled up close to him. She must have fallen asleep in the chair next to his bed, but her head is resting on the mattress now, close to his torso. Her arms splay out over his abdomen.

She's still asleep. Breathing evenly. He hesitates, not wanting to shatter this moment apart. He reckons he could drift away again to the soft sounds she makes as she sleeps.

Instead, he prods her. She jerks awake and ricochets away from him. The sudden absence of her presence leaves him feeling quite cold.

She paces around the hospital room. It's a small thing, but he notices there aren't any flowers or balloons. In the movies or on television, there are always flowers and balloons in hospital rooms.

"What happened to me?" he asks once the nurse departs, and he blinks his way back to reality.

She stops pacing and stretches her arms up, which causes her shirt to ride up her abdomen, revealing a patch of skin above her jeans. There's a sudden visceral memory of how she had once felt beneath his fingertips, but he doesn't indulge it. He can't. Instead, he tilts his head, and his vision finally sharpens. He knows now with certainty that they're in a hospital, just not which one. His arms are sore from the IV lines, and his mouth is still pretty dry.

"Well, someone found you passed out down by the wharf," she begins, speaking as she stretches, rubbing her neck. "They called an ambulance, and the EMTs called me from your phone because of the whole emergency contact thing. You were dehydrated and your blood sugar was critically low," she pauses, giving him a weighted look, "among other things."

Maybe not scare him with the gory details. Just yet.

"How do you know all this? Why did they tell you?"

She pauses, confused by his inquiry.

He clarifies. "Aren't there privacy issues? Why did they just tell you all this?"

Callie looks away from him. "Oh. I told them I'm your fiancée."

He tilts his head. "Fiancée. Not sister? Not cousin?"

She shrugs. "I called your mom, Alex," she adds, changing the subject. "She's coming soon."

"My dad?" He asks.

She narrows her eyes at him. "He's still in Vegas, where you left him without bail."

Oh right. That whole fiasco.

He lifts a hand to his face, where a bandage extends from his jaw up to his forehead.

"Your face hit a rock or something. It'll scar," she tells him, deadpan, as she watches him trace the outline of the bandage.

He winces. Guess that sealed the deal with his doomed fate as an Instagram model.

He looks at her. She comes back to his bedside and scoots the chair closer to him. She speaks and stops a few times, fumbling for her words. She's supposed to be the communicative one here, you see.

"Alex, remember what we were talking about the other night? About the universes?"

He nods, wondering where she's going with this. He's too drugged up to process anything that isn't surface deep.

"It's nice to think about that stuff. But I need you to understand me." She sighs, hoping she can communicate here. "You're in this universe. And maybe there's another universe where everything is okay, but that's not this one. So, make everything okay in this universe, because it's the only one you get to live in, right here, right now. Do it because nobody else will."

"I understand," he tells her. He's telling the truth. He understands. "And you're a *fucking* mess, Alex," she looks around at the beeping monitors. She's just stating facts. "But in this universe, you happen to have people who care about you."

And then she pulls away from him, and adds, "But you have to want to want it."

Their eyes meet, and the sight chills her along every nerve ending. His dark hair is stringy and spreads out across the rough pillow beneath his head. She wishes she had brought a better pillowcase for him.

"I don't know your entire story. I'm not telepathic..." she covers his hands with hers. "Anyway. Your mom should be here soon. She loves you, Alex," Callie tells him as she lifts his hand and presses her lips to his wrist. "So don't push her away. Please don't fuck this up."

His vision blurs, slowly. Creeping in like dripping paint on a canvas. Where is he again? His eyes slide closed.

"And if you want, you can find me here on the other side." He swears he hears her say this. It will play over and over in his head as he drifts in and out of sleep. What does it mean?

When he wakes up again, hours later, she's gone. The chair by his bedside is still there. He reaches an arm out for the cushion. The seat has gone cold.

A month later, Alex has a duffel bag slung over his shoulder, and his mother is pressing a plane ticket to his chest, pressing a kiss to his cheek.

"I'm meeting with the lawyer later today. And call me when you land?" Sandra asks him.

He nods, hesitating at the door. Outside, the taxi beeps.

"Mom, if you see Callie–"

Sandra nods at him, waving her hand. "Worry about you right now. Just go."

Once he settles into the taxi, he looks back over his shoulder, watching as his mother becomes a small dot and then disappears into the facade of the house behind her.

This part of his life will be a blur.

He'll just remember a maze made of stones placed in the grass. Walking around that maze a lot. It had felt out of character for him, at first. He will remember sitting cross-legged in a circle. A lot. There's something healing, apparently, about sitting cross-legged in a circle with other fucked up people.

He'll remember how time doesn't feel like it passes, but how one day is his first day and the next is his last. He'll remember how when he finally returns home and drops his duffel on the floor, it sounds like a bubble bursting.

The bubble bursts because time has passed, and things have changed. And because they don't tell you what to do now that everything has "gotten better".

They don't tell you it doesn't magically get better. That there's no switch to flip to bring everything else in your life up to speed. The switch doesn't exist.

But they tell you to take it one day at a time. So he does.

"I don't know what to do, but I know I need to talk to someone about stuff." she sits at the edge of the office chair. "And not my friends, if you know what I mean," she explains.

Haven smiles at her. "I know what you mean."

"I don't know how to go about that," she tells her. "But I might need some help. Someone to talk to. Is that okay?"

Haven nods with a smile. "It's all okay. We'll work it out."

This part of her life teaches her to cry in the arms of the people who care for her. This part of her life, above all other things, teaches her she doesn't have to run away. And that her story was never about to begin. She was, and always could be, just living it. So she does.

Chapter Twenty-Seven

One year later

"Hey."

She's locking up the studio for the night, yoga mat over her shoulder. She spins around, arms outstretched, fists clenched in a fighting stance.

"Oh, wow. Hi." Her muscles relax, but only slightly, at the familiar face. "Wow, hi."

Guess she couldn't avoid this forever, if he was, in fact, back in town. It had been a few days since she'd seen him slip into the studio.

"Hi."

"Hi?"

"I'm looking for my mom," Alex Bardot says with his hands in his pockets.

Callie shakes her head. "She normally clocks out hours before this. But she's on a weekend trip, with Haven."

"Oh."

"Where have you–" she asks, but the answer is in front of her. She only needs to look.

His hair is softer than she remembers and falls in waves around his face. She's maybe never seen it this well kept. His eyes are bright, white and clear. She's never seen them, not bloodshot. It's strange.

In fact, the dark circles that had seemed etched beneath his eyes are almost gone. He's not as muscular, but still fit, like a normal sort of jacked. He's wearing a button-down shirt, a crisp pair of khaki pants.

The answer is simple. She feels strange, saying it out loud. Acknowledging what had happened.

Acknowledging how he's *better*. It's likely not as simple as all that, but it's what she has to take at face value for now. And she figures, in time, maybe, she'll know the whole story.

Frustration coils deep in her stomach. Because he had disappeared. But maybe now's not the time to bring that up. The last time she saw him, he looked barely human, hooked up to so many tubes and wires. Again, she's just relieved to see him. She tells the fury and the memory of recent heartbreak to slow down.

"You look good, Alex." She says instead. He nods at her in thanks.

He looks over to High Octane to see it boarded up.

"I hear it's going to be a bookstore," she offers.

"It's the perfect space for that."

There's a beat of silence before he speaks again.

"I wanted . . . I was coming here to update my mom on legal stuff. You know. The contracts," he fidgets a bit. "I wasn't sure if I'd see you."

"Here I am," she motions with her hands.

They stand both light years–and yet only mere feet–apart. The words left unspoken hang heavy in the space between them.

"I'm, I was accepted to a grad program?" he offers, apropos of nothing. "Astrophysics at UCSB." He wants her to know.

"I got my GED," she blurts. Well, she'd gotten it a year ago. She should tell him now, better late than never. She wants him to know.

"You were working hard on that." He remembered.

"And I'm in undergrad now. I started a few months ago."

"Really? Where?"

She looks up at him and fiddles with the strap of her yoga mat. "Computer science. UCSB."

Realization crosses his face.

"I'm happy for you," they both say. In unison.

"Would you maybe . . . what if . . . would you like to grab coffee or something tomorrow afternoon? I have class at noon. But after?" There's that feeling again. It's either excitement or fear. But it makes her want to tear up all the same.

"I would like that," he offers. He ignores the visible tears glistening in her eyes.

"Right," she kicks a pebble at her feet. It skitters across the sidewalk.

"Alex, it's," she's on her toes, wrapping her arms around his broad shoulders in a hug. He's so warm, and she presses her head against his chest. He's real, he's here. He's back. "It's just good to see you. That's all."

There's a torrential downpour the next day. She's forgotten her umbrella. A decision she's regretted all day, more so now that her class is over and she has to hope her laptop is safe in her backpack.

She's standing outside the café where they agreed to meet, and he's ten minutes late. Callie keeps checking her phone under the protective awning of the shop. Peering through the glass windows of the cafe, she considers giving up.

He appears around the corner, soaking. His shirt is plastered to his skin.

"Where have you been?" she snaps at him. It's strange how easily she accuses him. But there's a familiarity to it.

Frankly, she's earned the right to roast him, after all this time. She also considers the whole count-to-ten thing she's been learning regarding anger, and identifying the feeling or whatever and communicating those feelings, but this is Alex we're talking about.

"I was," she lets out a huff of air, "I wasn't sure you were even going to show."

There's a thunderclap somewhere in the distance.

"We should go inside," he tells her, motioning towards the coffee shop.

They wander inside and order, standing an awkward distance apart before settling in at a rickety wooden table. It does the weird thing where it doesn't seem to balance on one side. Alex takes a moment to fiddle with the table's support system, bunching up a couple of napkins and shoving them under the feet. When this fails, he sighs and comes back up, resting his elbows on the table.

They stare at each other in silence. This felt like it should be much easier. It's not.

"Hi."

"Hey," she responds, sipping her cold brew through a straw. Neither of them have been to this cafe before. She keeps pretending to let her attention span get away from her, letting her eyes wander across the walls of the decorated walls. There doesn't seem to be a singular aesthetic or theme to this place. Maps of Southern California hang on the walls, paired with vintage typewriters resting on top shelves. Empty bottles of vintage liquor litter the windowsills. There are burlap sacks on the ground that she's convinced are filled with packing peanuts.

"So you're in college," he states. She nods in response and avoids meeting his eyes again.

"I am in college."

"That's great. I'm happy for you."

She wants to scream. She clenches her fists. He already said that. They've already said all this. There's nothing more they can say.

She remembers that kitten she had tried to nurse back to health all those years ago. The one that had run away after she had brought it back to her campsite. How heartbroken she had been the next morning when she found it had disappeared.

This feeling between them, just right now, felt something close to that. Not that Alex *was* the kitten. No, don't make this weird. Just the feeling. If she had to compare it to anything.

She's been working hard for the past year. Her friends and therapist say she has made progress. But no, she's not sure she can do this.

"I can't do this," she slams her cold brew down on the table. The unstable surface creaks beneath the weight of the flimsy plastic cup.

She gets up and storms out of the coffee shop into the pouring rain. *Don't follow me. Don't do it. I don't want to do this right now.*

Chapter Twenty-Eight

Her internal monologue mocks her. *Liar.*

He follows her, of course.

"Callie, it's okay, I get it, let's just talk–"

"No! I don't want to!" She crosses her arms over her chest and stomps her foot. "I don't have anything to say."

The constructed dam she had built deep within herself bursts open, and hell hath no fury like a chick with some repressed anger issues. Fuck counting to ten. Fuck mindfulness right now. A small place inside of her feels guilty and knows she'll be held accountable for this outburst later, maybe.

He takes a step towards her as if to comfort her, and she steps back, maintaining the space between them.

"I was there for you–" she says. She's on this horrible seesaw, balancing between running for the fucking Los Padres hills and, well, staying here. What a horrible sensation.

"Callie."

"You didn't have to do it alone." It's what she wants to say, maybe. But is it the truth?

"I did," he counters. She eyeballs him. "I did have to do it alone," he explains.

She gasps for breath, and she realizes her chest has been heaving.

It's then that she realizes that she just didn't want him to leave *her* alone, maybe. Maybe that's the truth. Ew, that's not a nice realization for her to come to, she decides. That feels more selfish than she wants to give herself credit for.

"I'm pissed off with the way you handled that," she snaps. Not to sound dramatic, but where do the tears end and the raindrops begin? "You could have called or something. Your mom could have said something to me. You could have said where you were going."

He steps closer to her again, but this time, she stands still. He stands there, unmoving, testing their proximity, his hair growing wetter by the second and falling in messy twirls around his face and over his forehead.

"Say something, jackass!" She yells, stomping her foot again. "Say anything! Don't just stand there!"

He blinks, before taking a step forward, closing the space between them only slightly. She exhales through her nose, wiping the back of her hand across her mouth as copious amounts of snot and raindrops and tears drip down her face. She's glad she didn't get particularly dolled up for this occasion.

He takes one more step, so close to her now, their torsos mere inches apart. She has to tilt her neck up to meet his gaze like this. It's fierce, and she's trying so hard not to blink, but the rain keeps getting in her eyes and stinging.

And then his hands, his huge behemoth goddamn paws, come up to clutch her cheeks. He runs his palms over her skin for a moment, smearing the rain across her skin before he lets his fingers run back and comb through her wet hair. She still stands there, fists clenched at her side.

"I think you broke my heart," she blurts, thinking out loud.

There's a moment of hesitation, as he nudges at the corner of what *he's* learned in the past year. Should he even be doing this? He hates how he's always second-guessing himself these days. But he doesn't want to wait another moment. Maybe he's impatient. He's been learning a lot about himself lately. Impatient sounds about right.

"Don't just–" she says but is cut off by his mouth. A very rude interruption by plush, warm lips and a soft, searching tongue.

Damn it.

And then, she pushes him away, her fists on his chest, and says: "Why *didn't* you just text me or something?"

What is this? A Nicholas Sparks scene?

He looks down at her, tilting his head. "Well." He pauses. He thinks about his words, how to say what he wants to say. "You said you'd be here on the other side." He hopes she gets it. Hope she remembers. Just hopes.

She looks at him, understanding.

And she does know all about waiting. It's just this time. Waiting seems to have had an outcome she could tolerate.

"So, is this the other side?" she asks with a hiccup.

He nods at her, but shrugs. "Is it ever the other side? Is there such a thing?"

She hiccups again with a laugh. They both know the answer to that.

He chuckles as well. "Let's try this again," he tells her.

"Try this again?"

He motions at the space between them. He takes a very deep breath. Because shit is about to get real. Because life is messy. People, in particular, are messy.

He inhales, thinks for a moment he might choke on a raindrop, and remembers how in another life, his hands may have trembled. They're steady now.

"You made me want to be better," he states.

She tilts her head up at him. "What?"

"Callie, I fell in love with you," he clarifies. When he says this, her mouth falls open, and rain falls onto her lips and tongue. She considers the effects of acid rain. He continues. "I began to love you through every paleo delivery. I loved you every time you pulled your hair into a ponytail. In fact, I do love this, right here." he reaches a hand out to caress the hair at the nape of her neck. "And I had to set all that aside for a while. But loving you is what made me want to be better."

There's lightning in the sky. This doesn't seem safe. Should they move back under the cafe awning, at least? But he continues, as she blinks raindrops out of her eyes and tries to just focus on her breathing. Her heart rate has sped up a bit.

"I loved you even when you yelled at me." He has to raise his own voice a little as the downpour gets a little louder. "Even now. I have loved you when you licked ice cream off my face. I have loved you even though you eat your pizza the wrong way." She crosses her arms at that. He continues with a fervor. "I love how you're a firecracker. You are stubborn. I love that. You are persistent. I have loved you when you wrestled me, I have loved you when you're in my arms and when you're not here, Callie, you're everything to me."

He takes another deep breath, trying not to choke on the downpour. "And Callie, god damn it, I still love you. And I can't let that go unsaid, not for another day."

She blinks. Well, this was an improvement in the communication department. She's not sure even she could be that verbose. She sobs, helpless, still caught up. Feeling like she had missed out on something critical.

"I could have been there," she tries again. "I could have–helped–"

He shuts her up with another kiss. "And if you'll have me, Callie, if you'll have me, we can do this again. I'm sorry I never said it before. I'm sorry. Now, I am saying it. We can do it again and I can do this right this time, if you'll let me love you. If you'll let me love you," he says, before sighing and lowering his voice to a whisper that slides into a tearful plea. "Let me love you."

She sobs harder now. Her hands twist into his wet hair as she cries.

Chapter Twenty-Nine

They stumble back into her cottage, knocking things over and fumbling.

She laughs as his breath tickles her neck.

They collapse on her bed and they laugh together.

He's the warmest thing she's ever felt. She's the softest thing he's ever touched.

And then things slow down, like a like a slow stop-motion video, and everything gets careful.

It gets fucking slow.

He peels off her shirt, up and over her head, maintaining eye contact with her. They aren't smiling now, but they're unable to stop looking at each other.

She can count every speckle in his eyes. How she had grown so accustomed to the twitch in his lower lid, no longer present. He can see every wrinkle surrounding hers. There's maybe three more now than he remembered. Since the last time he saw her. He thinks about the time he flew over the Grand Canyon once, long ago, and how her eyes look like all the ridges and colors of that landscape.

He exhales. She reaches back to unclasp her bra and follows by lifting his shirt up over his head.

And he pulls her close, pressing her skin to his skin.

His hands flatten against her upper back so that he can hold her here, so close, so that he can trick his mind into losing where he ends, and she begins.

She circles her arms around to pull him close as well. Her arms don't quite reach his upper back, but it's enough.

They embrace each other. Chest to chest, hands to back, holding each other for god knows how long. He just wants to feel her everywhere. Because, he's decided, she's everywhere to him, in every universe.

"I love you," she tests it. It feels like she's just laying the groundwork for something new inside her. She's the architect of this new thing within her soul. Maybe she can let him in, to whatever this new thing is she's ready to build again.

They fall back on the bed, tangling themselves together, legs stacked over each other. His arm holding her in close so that she can tuck her head into his chest.

"Is this okay?" she wonders out loud, her breath tickling his collarbone. "For people like us?"

"There will always be people like us." He pulls away from her a bit so that he can meet her gaze. "So why not?"

She cries and doesn't stop crying. They hold each other. The rain pitter-patters against the window of her bedroom.

"You came back," she mumbles through the tears that won't stop.

And hours later, they wake up. It's morning. They begin to kiss each other.

Neither of them even notices the morning breath on the other's tongue.

He slides a hand down between her legs, he kisses her neck the way he knows she likes, and she rocks against his fingers.

He lifts the sheets up and over them both.

And then, cupping her face and pressing a kiss to her forehead, he enters her, agonizingly slow. Her lips part as she lets out a soft sigh at the sensation.

They rock together for a few moments, or maybe for hours? Who knows? But they don't look away from each other for a second.

And they kiss an obscene amount, and he kisses her neck and every inch of skin he can get his lips on. Because he can't stand any part of him that's not touching her.

He's realized that there are so many ways to touch and be touched like so many words on a page. Like the alphabet and dictionary and all the ways to arrange words into prose. He could touch her and be touched by her in a new way every time, each way with a different meaning, a different weight, a different tone.

Millions and millions of different combinations, even if it's gibberish, even if it makes perfect sense.

And she rolls them over so she can be on top. She can feel him deep within her, and she tilts her body down over his and presses her chest to his and rocks against him. The endorphins overtake them both, and it makes perfect sense.

She comes as she's looking into his eyes. Her hands go to slide through his hair and she tries to map out the changes of color in his irises as her climax spreads throughout every inch of her veins and arteries and capillaries.

It doesn't take him long after that. His hands come up to pull her mouth down to his, to kiss her as he gasps when he comes as well.

They roll over on their sides. He's still inside her, and they stay like that, her leg tossed over his thigh, their chests pressed close together. His hands in her hair. Her arms around his torso, pulling him close in every universe.

"You came back."

About the Author

USA Today & International Best Selling Author Ashley Zakrzewski is known for her captivating storytelling, sultry plots, and dynamic protagonists. Hailing from Arkansas, her affinity for the written word began early on, and she has been relentlessly chasing after her dreams ever since.

You can find signed copies of her books here and sign up for her newsletter.

www.ashleyzakrzewski.com

Made in the USA
Middletown, DE
18 November 2024

64772774R00094